Robins on
The Red River

AN EMMA HAINES KAYAK MYSTERY

Trudy Brandenburg

D1715641

Photo Cover: The Red River, Kentucky
Photograph by Trudy Brandenburg

ROBINS ON THE RED RIVER
V2017
Copyright © 2015 by Trudy Brandenburg
TAB Productions, L.L.C.
All rights reserved.

ISBN-13: 9781546334859
ISBN-10: 1546334858

Dedicated to
Steve Earley
and
David "Cappy" Caplinger

Paddle. Paddle. Paddle.

Chapter I

THE MAN STOOD on the bridge above the Red River in Kentucky, watching Emma Haines and Stratton Reeves paddle downstream in their kayaks. He lowered the high-powered binoculars, turned, and walked toward his truck.

Emma paddled her blue Perception America kayak named *Arlene* upstream toward her beau, Stratton Reeves. She named her kayak after her friend Arlene who lost her battle to cancer.

"You have a key to your truck, right?" she asked.

"I do. After the last time I had one made and keep it right here in my life jacket pocket. See?" The Velcro ripped open as he lifted the pocket and showed her the key on the ring that was sewn onto the jacket.

She turned her boat, and they paddled lazily downstream. Stratton looked up at the walls of the gorge. "This is beautiful country."

"Yeah. Charles and I fell in love with this place the first time we paddled it with SOFA about ten years ago. After that, the two of us came here every year on this weekend."

SOFA stood for the Southern Ohio Floaters Association, based out of Emma's hometown of Chillicothe, Ohio. She and her friend Charles Wellington often paddled with the group.

"It's a fun river, and there's a nice little class two rapid a few miles from the take-out that we can surf." She paused as they paddled toward a bend in the river and looked up. "Like I told you, rock climbers come here from all over the world to scale the cliffs. Check that out." She pointed at a majestic rock wall ahead of them. Its bald face rose above the green buds of the forest. A cloud floated behind the mountaintop, highlighting a small stand of pine trees.

She turned her attention to the left, where a boulder several stories tall sat in the stream. "Can you imagine the noise the glaciers made grinding their way over the earth and pushing things like that around?"

"I've never thought of the sounds before. That's a good point. Those were probably like marbles to the glaciers," he said.

Dead trees, logs, and sticks—which kayakers refer to as "junk"—were piled against several trees along the shore. It was another reminder of recent flooding and the power of water.

"Hey, let me get your picture," she said. "It'll make a desktop shot for sure. I'll paddle back upstream and you sit in the middle of the river so I can get the boulder and the mountain behind you." She paddled past him, then turned her boat.

"Whatever you say, Ms. Photographer." He paddled to the middle of the stream and turned his kayak to face her. He sat tall resting his paddle across the cockpit. He wore a huge smile on his morning-shaven face. A pair of Oakley sunglasses sat on his nose under the brim of his *Stonefalls Post* ball cap. Emma gave the glasses to him for his sixty-fifth birthday in November. She thought the sunglasses made him look more handsome—if that were possible.

Sky Bridge Road ran just above them, along the top of the ridge. She adjusted the shot so it wouldn't appear in the picture. She tapped the camera icon on her iPhone through the water-proof case, which had been a Christmas gift from Charles. She lowered the phone and paddled toward Stratton. He turned his boat, and they continued downstream.

"Do we really need to leave this afternoon? I know you want to get back to Clintonville, but can't we at least stay the night? We've already paid for the cabin," he said.

She put her phone in her life jacket pocket and looked his way, scrunching her face. "I really want to get back tonight. Calvin has another claims group for me to speak to, and I want to review the presentation before Monday. I can't help it he moved the meeting up a week. At least we still got to paddle here."

"There's Wi-Fi and cell reception in the cabin. You should've brought your laptop."

She frowned. "You know I never bring my laptop on trips, and it will be easier if I wake up at home in the morning. I planned on staying, but we'll be at the take-out in about three hours. If we drive straight to the cabin and get our stuff and leave, we can be home by nine. Save me time tomorrow. I want to run their investigative methods by Joey tomorrow, too."

Joey Reed was a detective on the police force back in Emma's hometown of Clintonville, Ohio, and a good friend.

They cracked many cases together while she worked at Matrix Insurance as a fraud investigator. He helped her bust a couple of perps on two recent kayak trips, too, one while she and Charles were kayaking on the New River in West Virginia last July and the second in October while they were kayaking on Paint Creek, near Chillicothe. Stratton had helped her with that case and had been taken a stray bullet. Thankfully, it was just a scratch.

They paddled in silence through the steep valley. Huge rocks and cliffs peeked out from the hillsides. The bright blooming purple of redbud trees and white dogwood blossoms popped with color throughout the green of the budding woods. Wildflowers dotted the hillsides stretching toward the Kentucky sun.

"Emma, do you really need to work so much?"

"I do if I want to keep paying Merek to run my business so I can kayak with you whenever I want. You know, I'm tired of having this conversation." She turned her boat downstream and paddled ahead of him.

Stratton followed her. His paddle left swirls in the water. She slowed and waited for him, and they paddled beside each other. "Look," Emma said, pointing downstream. A snake slithered across the river in front of them. "I love the way they swim."

"Snakes—" A clap of thunder interrupted him. They both looked toward the sky. Several turkey vultures circled overhead.

"I checked the weather and the storms were not supposed to drop down this far," she said.

Stratton turned in his seat. The sky was dark behind them. "Probably just going to go around us. I'm hungry. Let's stop for lunch."

"Your never-ending appetite amazes me."

"I have to maintain my strength to keep up with you, my dear," he said with a hint of sarcasm.

She rolled her eyes.

They paddled onto a small rocky beach, got out of their boats, and took their lunch bags from the boat cockpits. They tossed their life jackets and paddles on their seats, walked to a log, and sat down.

"I hope you like your PB&Js. I made them just the way you like them—a little P and lots of J," she said. She bit into her sandwich wondering—once again—how Stratton ate so much and stayed in such great shape.

"I'm sure they're fine," he said, not looking at her. They ate and enjoyed the scenery.

"Something wrong?" she asked.

He finished chewing before he said, "I'm not sure I should leave for the reporters' conference in Texas next week."

"Why not?"

He chewed more and swallowed. "Emma, you know they haven't caught Earl Calhoon."

She shrugged. "So?"

"So? You're the one that put him in prison again, and he probably doesn't like you very much. That's what's so. Stop acting so naïve."

5

She bit off a piece of her sandwich before she looked away. A robin bounced along the water's edge in front of them. Moments later, another robin ran beside it.

"You ever notice how similar male and female robins look? You can't tell the difference. I think I read the male's a little brighter-colored than the female," she said.

"Please don't ignore the conversation."

"You know, I'm tired of having this conversation, too. What am I supposed to do about Calhoon? Keep worrying about him and looking over my shoulder the rest of my life? I've put several very bad guys away. I can't worry about it. It's all part of the job. You know that. I'm sure you made enemies as a hot-shot crime reporter back in the day. I can take care of myself. I did for years before I met you. You've gone back home for weeks and left me alone," she snapped.

Emma had Earl-the-Pearl Calhoon imprisoned when she and Charles were kayaking in Stonefalls, West Virginia, after they accidentally met him on the river last July. But Calhoon had escaped and was still on the loose.

That's when she also met the handsome *Stonefalls Post* newspaper owner Stratton Reeves who fell in love with the forty-four-year-old, spunky, petite, brunette at first sight. Her tenacious independence both attracted and recently frustrated him. Sometimes their twenty-year age difference caused ripples in their otherwise calm relationship.

Stratton stood and walked to the water's edge. He turned toward her, "It frightens me how nonchalant you are about certain things." He turned back around and faced the river.

"Guess that's just how this little girl rolls," she grumbled toward his back.

They ate their lunch. The stream gurgled, and a cardinal sang in a tree across the river. A chickadee fussed above them as it pounded a seed against a limb. An oriole called out several times as a burst of wind rocked the treetops. The branches clacked together in a crazy dance. One of the larger trees creaked as it swayed.

She took a long swig from the red metal water bottle her friend Sue had given her years ago. All the scratches and dents from being banged on boats, trees, and rocks made it extra special. It was her good luck charm on the rivers. She screwed the cap on the bottle and stared at Stratton's back.

He was the first man in years who stopped her in her tracks when she met him. Over the past ten months, things had moved along quickly between them. They spent so much time together that he moved into her condo around Christmas.

They were getting along fine, except for recent tiffs. Stratton wanted to play more. Emma wanted to work more. And for the life of her, she really didn't understand why. Stratton had told her they didn't have to work another day in their lives, but the thought of it frightened her and made her want to work harder.

Ahead of them the sky was blue, filled with white puffy clouds. A distant roll of thunder drifted through the valley behind them, and the sky was slightly gray. Another gust of wind brought a drop in the temperature. A large branch crashed to the ground behind them.

"The river's rising and the temperature's falling," he said, gazing upstream.

"That it is," she said.

A burst of wind caused the trees to sway. Two cardinals, a great blue heron, and a kingfisher chattered as they flew downstream like they were fleeing a predator.

"We better get going," he said, walking past her to his boat, its stern beginning to float on the rising water. He put his lunch in the cockpit, put on his life jacket, and sat in his kayak.

"Did you bring your rain gear?" she asked.

He shook his head. "It's in the truck."

She always kept rain gear and a spray skirt in her boat and had suggested he do the same. "You're going to freeze, and your boat's going to fill with water if it starts to rain hard. If it gets bad, we should wait it out," she said.

"I'll be fine," he said, waving her comment away. "Let's keep going. Paddling will keep me warm. I think it'll pass by us."

She looked at the blue sky ahead of them and the graying sky behind them. It could go around them. She checked the weather before they left the cabin, and only a slight chance of pop-up storms had been predicted.

She walked to her boat, pulled her rain gear out of the cockpit, and shoved her lunch bag back in it. She put on her rain pants and jacket, stepped into her spray skirt, and tightened it around her waist. She shrugged on her life jacket, sat back down in her boat, and rolled the spray skirt edges over the lip of the cockpit. They pushed off into the water and started downstream.

Thirty minutes later it began to sprinkle.

They paddled around the sharp curve below the abandoned Pumpkin Bottom campground. A sudden burst from the sky, and rain streamed from the brims of their ball caps as if pitchers of water were being poured on their heads. They could barely see past the front of their kayaks. The stream was rising fast and picking up speed. They kept their heads low, straining to see.

Emma had paddled in worse storms, but this one was bad and she worried about Stratton. He hadn't kayaked much and wasn't dressed for this. She doubted he had paddled in any storm.

A bolt of lightning lit the sky as if a bomb had exploded. She gasped.

"We need to get off this river! Now!" she yelled over her right shoulder.

"Okay! The next place we can pull over!" he yelled, looking to his left with his hand on the bill of his ball cap. "I don't see any place along here."

"Stratton! Strainer!" She paddled hard left around a tree bobbing in the river, the current pulling them toward it.

Stratton's kayak hit a limb and rolled. He fell out of the boat and was sucked under the tree.

"No! No! No!" she screamed as she fought the water to find a place to pull over, looking for an eddy along the bank.

But the current moved her fast downstream. She turned her boat to try to paddle upstream, but the river pushed her back. She couldn't see through the rain. Stratton's boat and paddle shot past her in the water.

The water flipped her bow downstream and she paddled hard, going with it rather than fighting it. The wind blasted, and two trees crashed into the river in front of her. She dodged them, digging her paddle in the water and making tight turns as she braced her legs against the walls of her kayak. Her heart pounded.

She took a deep breath and yelled, "Come on, *Arlene*. We have to get off this river. Help me!"

As she approached the only rapid on the river, whitecaps rose in front of her like the long white fingers of a ghost. It wasn't the small rocky thrill that she and Charles always enjoyed. It looked like a raging white monster. The riverbank had disappeared, and water lapped at the trees along the steep hillsides. She had to get off this river. But first she had to get through this rapid.

She pointed *Arlene's* bow straight into the white wave that rose in front of her like a giant claw. "Come on, *Arlene*. We can do this!" she yelled as the wave crashed over the front of *Arlene* and slapped onto the spray skirt. *Arlene* dropped down into a hole, popped out, and hit another wave. Emma had to keep the kayak straight or she'd roll, dump, and be swept downstream. She squinted from under her ball cap, biting her lip, breathing hard.

She paddled fast, adrenaline rushing through her strong one-hundred thirty-pound body.

On the other side of the rapid she raised her head, leaned forward, and put her paddle in the water along the right bow of her boat near her feet. *Arlene* turned a hard right and sat bobbing in an eddy facing upstream.

Emma let out a sigh of relief. But as she examined the bank beside her there wasn't a place to get out of the kayak. The water lapped several feet above the bank against the trees, and the hillside went straight up. Even if it had been a small incline, it would be slick and hard to gain footing.

The eddy she caught behind a set of boulders was disappearing fast under the rising river. The rapid she just paddled through was at least a Class III at this point, normally a small Class I ripple. In river-speak, a Class I is easy-paddling water and Class V the most difficult.

A blast of wind rocked her boat. "We have to get off this river," she said to *Arlene*.

She floated backward downstream several feet and studied the area. It was getting more difficult to keep *Arlene* pointed upstream on the rising water as it started splashing over the rocks that were guarding them from the current.

She shook her head to get the rain from her eyes and looked up the bank again. A tree hung over her, but not in reach. Just above the tree, a small, rocky ravine gushed water. If she could get out of her boat, she could stand in the ravine.

She turned the boat downstream, then back upstream. The rocks she and *Arlene* were hiding behind were nearly gone and Emma had a hard time staying in the disappearing eddy, but she could nearly grab the branch of a tree. She found a small spot and paddled the nose of the kayak between two rocks and sat bobbing in the water.

"I'll find you later. I promise," she yelled to *Arlene*. She held her paddle in her left hand and reached down and popped her spray skirt from the cockpit with her right. She stood, balancing in the kayak for a split second before she crouched in the boat and used the branch to pull herself into the ravine. She gained her footing and turned toward *Arlene* to see if she might be able to grab the bow handle. But the boat was too far away and she didn't want to risk falling into the river.

As if to say farewell, *Arlene*'s bow bounced free from the rocks, faced Emma, and swayed in the water several times before it was pushed by the current. Emma's heart sank as *Arlene* floated downstream and disappeared.

Stratton tumbled in the tree limbs like he was in a front-load washing machine. He grabbed the branches and pulled hard several times, straightening his body in line with the current.

He couldn't hold his breath any longer. *I'm not going to drown in this tree.* He pulled hard and shot up on the other side of the tree, holding onto the branches. He gulped air into his aching lungs. His body flew out behind him, and he almost lost his grip. He pulled his torso up on top of the tree, but his legs were being pulled downstream into the current. He took a deep breath and heaved himself onto the branches.

He lay sprawled on the tree on his stomach and watched the raging river flow through the tree under him. The rain beat on him like tiny hammers. He raised his head and got his bearings. He would have to make his way up the tree to land. And hurry. The tree was pulling away from the bank.

He turned toward the woods, leaned forward, and crawled along the tree on his stomach, pushing himself with his legs like a soldier crawling through the mud. A memory from Vietnam flashed into his mind, and he shoved it down. *I survived then, and I'll survive now.*

The branches and bark cut and scratched his legs through his thin pants and slit his arms and hands. Once he got to the trunk of the tree he clawed and climbed up the muddy root ball and sat on top of it, catching his breath. Blood seeped through his torn pants and trickled down his face and arms. Water rose between the root ball and the bank and the current picked up speed, pushing the treetop. Suddenly, it lurched free from the bank and swung downstream.

"Ahhhhrgh!"

He toppled from the root ball and plunged into the water. He gasped and grabbed a limb from another tree and pulled himself up the slick bank, holding onto roots and branches, clawing at the ground, and climbing on his hands and knees.

Once above the water line he turned and sat down. The tree he stood on spun as it was swept away like a twig.

He wiped away mud, blood, and leaves from himself, stood, and started climbing the steep bank toward the main road on the ridge. He had to find Emma.

When Stratton reached the edge of the road the rain was a sprinkle, making the leaves in the woods dance as the drops bounced on them. Birds began to sing.

He unzipped his life jacket, took it off, and hung it from a small tree. He dug into the left pocket, worked the truck key off the ring, and slid it into his pants pocket. As he reached for his life jacket he felt a sharp jab in his ribs that made him gasp and jerk straight up.

"You won't be needing that life jacket. We'll be taking a little ride. Put your hands in the air, make a right on the road, and keep walking until I tell you to stop at the truck. If you try to run I'll shoot you," a man's voice said with a slight accent.

Stratton stood fast.

A harder jab. "Now, Mr. Reeves. Or I'll shoot you where you stand."

Chapter 2

EMMA SAT UNDER a large pine tree. "Unbelievable," she whispered. The river had risen at least four feet since she and Stratton had started their trip from under the bridge.

The thunder rumbled in the distance, and the sky cleared. It sprinkled as she crawled from under the tree limbs. If she were on the north bank she could walk up the mountainside to the main road and hitch a ride. But she walked along the south bank of the river with no way to cross. She had to make her way through the forest to the footbridge that crossed the river, start walking toward her truck, and flag down any passing driver to help her. *Maybe Stratton will pick me up.*

After what seemed like forever, she walked along Sky Bridge Road, which paralleled the Red River. Rays of sunshine beamed through the trees like white lasers. The woods glistened and smelled of clean green and wet dirt. Raindrops dripped from the leaves, and a breeze lifted her small ponytail as a rainbow emerged over the river. She admired it as she walked.

A low engine noise floated through the valley, followed by the sound of hissing tires. *Maybe that rainbow was a sign.*

A black truck appeared over a rise, and her heart leapt into her throat. *Stratton*. But it wasn't Stratton's black Silverado pickup. *Maybe I can catch a ride*. She waved.

A shining tall GMC pickup that looked as if it were built for a monster truck show came to a stop in front of her. The windshield and windows were tinted so black that she couldn't see inside. Water dripped from the silver cow-kicker grille, as if it were drooling. The truck had no front plate. She waved and walked toward it.

Stratton sat in the passenger seat of the black monster truck. His hands sat in his lap bound with duct tape and the safety belt held him against the seat. A pair of binoculars lay on the console between him and the driver.

Emma walked toward them smiling and waving. She held her paddle in her right hand. Her life jacket hung open and she still wore her spray jacket, pants, and gloves.

He sat up straight as his heart lifted. He glanced at the driver then back at Emma. As she approached the driver turned the truck toward her.

"What are you doing?" Stratton asked. They sat in the truck. Emma walked toward it. The driver gunned the gas.

"Noooooooooo! Stop! Stop!" Stratton yelled, lurching and jerking in the seat as if he were being electrocuted while trying to swing at the driver with his bound fists.

The truck plowed over her before it fishtailed up the road and straightened.

Stratton looked in the side mirror. Emma lay in the middle of the road.

He sat speechless and numb, staring at the floorboard, breathing hard.

He raised his head and looked at his captor's profile. "You just ran over a woman, and you're smiling? What the hell kind of man are you?" Stratton sneered at the driver, tears running down his cheeks.

"A very rich and vengeful man, Mr. Reeves."

"How do you know my name? Who are you?"

"You're the award-winning newspaper reporter. You've written for papers all over the world and now you own a worthless rag in West Virginia called the *Stonefalls Post*. And you're the lover of that dead Emma Haines. Although this isn't how I planned it, I just couldn't help myself," he replied, glancing in his side mirror.

"Who are you?" Stratton demanded.

"You tell me, Mr. Award-winning reporter."

The man turned toward Stratton and removed his sunglasses. Their eyes locked for several seconds before the stranger pulled the truck over along the side of the road and jammed the gearshift into park. He pulled a syringe from his shirt pocket and stuck it in Stratton's arm.

Stratton's brow wrinkled and his eyes rolled back in his head. "What? Why? Why would you ... want to kill ... Emma?

Emma blinked her eyes. A blue sky peeked through budding tree limbs. She took a quick pain inventory, wiggled her fingers and toes, and bent her arms and legs. She rolled over, got up on her hands and knees, and stood. She walked to her paddle,

17

picked it up, and used it like a walking stick as she made her way over the hillside to hide.

She had dropped hard on the road, shut her eyes, and pulled her arms down next to her sides, placing her left cheek on the wet pavement as if she were being placed into a cannon.

She stood behind a tree and threw up. She walked further into the woods.

Her face was bleeding, and her bottom hurt. Other than that, she didn't feel physically injured. Her gloves, spray gear, and life jacket had protected her. She began shaking and slid down against a tree. The river roared below her, and she dropped her head back and sobbed.

She pulled herself together, anger replacing shock. She climbed up the ridge back onto the road and continued toward her truck, staying near the trees in case the black truck returned.

A beat-up green Subaru Outback pulled to a stop beside her. A kid wearing camo opened the window, and a wall of marijuana smoke nearly knocked Emma off her feet. He offered her a ride. She looked inside, and two other young men waved at her. "I just need a ride down the road to where my boyfriend fell out of his kayak." She decided to get her truck later.

"Hey, there. Hop in. I'm Toby. This is Josh," he pointed at the driver. "And that ugly dude in the back is Derek."

"Hey, man. Like, who you callin' ugly?" Derek laughed, a stoner's grin plastered on his face.

She studied the men again and climbed in, wedging her kayak paddle between the breaks in the back and front seats. She told them what had happened.

Derek dug out a first aid kit from a backpack and cleaned Emma's cheek while she talked. Although they said they passed a few vehicles, they didn't remember the black pickup. Not surprisingly, no one had cellphone reception.

"But the truck was huge. You couldn't have missed it," she said. "It had one of those big silver grilles that stick out on the front over the regular grille. The windows were black. And it didn't have a front plate. It sat about four feet off the ground."

"Sorry, man. I wasn't paying much attention," Toby answered through a brown shaggy beard and a crooked smile. "You guys?"

"No, man," Derek said, shaking his head, putting a bandage on Emma's cheek. She thanked him.

"There's lots of trucks here, man. They all look the same. Sorry," Josh replied, turning around in the front seat.

Emma figured they probably hadn't noticed much of anything. "Well, if you do see one, get the plates and call the sheriff. If it's got a plate, it'll be on the back."

Toby scowled at her in the rearview mirror with a look of "You've got to be kidding."

Emma peered out the side window. "It's along here, I think. Here. Here. Pull over. I'll get out here."

"You sure, man?" Toby asked.

"Yeah, this is it. You guys go to the lodge and call for help like we talked about, okay? Please? Just turn around and set your odometer and tell them where you dropped me off. And make sure you call the sheriff and tell them to look for Stratton and that black truck. If you see it, get the plate number and tell them what I told you. Don't go near the driver. He's crazy and dangerous. And if you see Stratton, tell him I'm okay and I'll meet him at the cabin."

"Sure thing, man. Wow. Dude ran over you on purpose. Wow, man. That's like nuts. And that's a bummer about your boyfriend. I hope he's okay," Toby said.

She gave them a sad smile. "He's a tough old bird. He'll be fine. Thanks for the ride," she said, opening the passenger door, doubting they would give the situation a second thought after they drove away.

She stepped out of the Subaru with her kayak paddle, shut the door, and walked toward the river. The car idled on the road. Derek and Josh got out with their climbing ropes draped over their shoulders. The Outback pulled along the side of the road and parked. Toby got out and followed, also carrying a rope.

"We're gonna help ya, Emma," Toby yelled.

"Hey, thanks, guys. Really. I appreciate it. Just don't fall in that river."

"Wow, man. Like that thing is totally screamin'," Derek yelled above the river noise.

"Raging, dude. Totally," Josh agreed.

"So you know why you can't fall in there," she yelled, staring at the river, her heart thudding in her throat. *Please don't let him be in that river.*

"Right. We'll rope up to some trees and rappel down."

"That's a great idea, but I'm a kayaker. I can't rappel. I thought about sliding down on my butt." The thought of doing that made her wince.

"No, man, you don't need to do that. We'll help you," Josh said.

"I can't thank you guys enough."

"It's cool. We just couldn't leave ya hangin', man."

The four of them made their way downhill through the woods on ropes they tied to trees along the roadway. Water dripped from the forest and puffy clouds floated through the blue sky—a beautiful afternoon. Below them the river roared, carrying trees and debris like toothpicks on rolling waves. They moved carefully down the slick hillside, slipping and sliding on the wet rocks and leaves.

When they got as close to the river as they dared, Emma hugged a tree and surveyed the area.

"Where's the tree?" Josh yelled.

"It was right there. I know it," she said, pointing at a hole in the riverbank where it once stood. Her heart sank.

"Hey, man. What's that?" Toby said. His back faced them and the river as he pointed up the hill toward the road. They followed his gaze up the mountainside several yards beyond the Outback.

Stratton's life jacket swayed on a branch of a small tree.

Merek banked his Harley into the curve coming down Route 374 through the Hocking Hills area. Fantasy hugged his waist, her face buried against his neck. Her blonde hair flew from beneath her helmet as they glided over the road.

They hiked through Ash Cave, eaten the picnic lunch she packed for them, hiked more, and were now on their way to

Merek's high-rise, Clintonville condo along the Olentangy River. They would hop into his king-size bed for a bit, shower, and then head to the Wildflower Café to eat the Saturday night fried chicken special—Merek's favorite.

Two hours later, Fantasy and Merek stared at his bedroom ceiling. "You know, you're different than the rest," she said.

He didn't answer. He knew he wasn't like most men that went into The Messenger Club, but he, too, liked to watch the beautiful ladies dance on the bar and strip. He checked the digital clock—8:30 p.m.

"Did you hear me?"

"*Tak.*"

"That means yes, right?"

"Yes. To you, in English, it means yes. I tell you that all the time. I know I am different. I am not a rich, married lawyer or a politician or a cop, like Joey. And," he paused, "I am from Poland." He smiled proudly.

"I'm not talking about *that.* I mean, I like the different way you talk and all, but I'm talking about you—about us. Me and you. You're different. You're special. I don't date the clients. And I'm not a badge bunny."

He turned his head toward her and gave her a disbelieving scowl.

"What? I don't. Well, okay, maybe once or twice. Until they wanted me to stop working."

"It is your job. Why would they want you to stop working?"

"Oh, honey. See, you are different from American men. That's why I love you so much."

She snuggled into him.

"We should go," he said.

"You're hungry."

"*Tak*."He laughed and patted his tight stomach. He was spending extra time at the gym, and it was paying off.

"You want to go eat fried chicken more than being with me?"

"You are not coming?" He grinned.

"Why don't I just cook something here and I'll feed you in bed," she whispered, running a red fingernail over his chest.

"You can fix breakfast in the morning." He gave her a peck on the check, threw his legs over the bed, and walked across the room to the bathroom door. She watched him as if she were looking at a piece of moving art. With the colorful tattoos over most of his torso, neck, arms and hands—she was.

Fantasy propped herself on an elbow. "So what's it like being a partner in a real business?"

He shrugged into his robe and tightened the sash. He turned to her. "You always ask me about my job. I do not want to talk about work today. I thought we agreed."

"Oh, okay. It's just that I always wanted my own business. You know, not taking orders from anyone. Wear expensive business suits and high heels and pantyhose to work. Be smart and fancy and pretty. Work in an office."

"You are smart and beautiful. You have a good job. Why do you want a different job?"

"I want a job where I can keep my clothes on and work around smart people. Some of those girls are just so dumb, and the manager is crazy. This is all I've done since I was sixteen. I don't know how to do anything else, and I always wanted to try."

"So you try. Why can you not try?"

She flopped back on the pillows. "I'm not good enough to do anything but be a stripper. That's why."

He walked over to her and pointed a finger. "That is an excuse. You want to do something, you try. I want to come to America. I tried. I did. You can, too."

She sat up. Her face was red. "How dare you speak to me like that. What do you think I can do?" She turned away from him.

"Go to college during the day. Work at night."

"Ha! That's a laugh. I can't afford to go to college. Besides, I don't think I can."

"Why can't you go to school? Everyone can go to college. Get a loan. Pay it off when you get a new job."

She was silent for a long moment. "I'd have to get my GED first," she said softly and started to cry. She jumped from the bed and ran past him into the bathroom, slamming the door behind her.

He stood staring at the door when his Samsung rang. He stomped to the bedside table, shaking his head. *I am not in the mood for this.* He picked up the phone.

"Hey, Miss H."

"Merek, Stratton took a swim from his boat in the river and we can't find him. And I was purposely run over by a truck.

Could you call Charles and both of you please come down here? And call Joey, too. Now?"

Charles sat on his deck in the back of his two-thousand square-foot rental home in Clintonville, watching his three adopted rescue Labrador retrievers—Sam, Cleo, and Cecil—romp and play in the backyard. The dogs were referred to as "the boys" by friends and family.

"That's right. Bring it here. Get it, Cecil. Sam, let Cecil bring it this time." He sipped a glass of Samuel Adams Utopias from a crystal beer glass and laughed as Cecil bounded onto the deck and dropped the Frisbee in his lap. The three dogs stood staring at him, tails wagging, tongues lolling from their mouths.

"Cleo, your turn," he said, flinging the Frisbee back out into the yard. The dogs ran after it, barking. Charles laughed again. "Get it." He took another sip of his beer and stretched out in the lounge chair. He closed his eyes, enjoying the warm breeze. He smoothed his gray mustache and flexed his long toes. It was only the second time he wore a pair of shorts, T-shirt, and sandals since last fall and he loved the feeling.

"Ahhhhhh. What a wonderful day."

This was his first Saturday at home in months, and he had no plans except to relax the entire weekend. *What should I prepare for dinner?*

He declined Emma's offer to go kayaking with her and Stratton. He didn't want to be a third wheel. He missed their being together, but since she met Stratton, their friendship had changed, as expected. He was happy for her. The *I-do-not-need-a-man-to-be-happy* woman was smitten with the handsome widower Stratton Reeves. And why wouldn't she be? If Stratton were gay, Charles would ask him out. Frankly, he wouldn't be surprised if she married him. Something he never thought Emma would do, but life changes people.

He leaned back in the chair, threaded his fingers, and put them behind his head. "I'm not going to leave this house until Monday morning."

Hopefully, when he got to work on Monday he wouldn't have many meetings—a rare event—or have to fire an engineer or save a satellite from crashing to Earth—his normal job duties.

After graduating from college nearly thirty-two years ago, he became the chief engineer at Bridge Systems. He had an international security clearance a mile long and a staff of over two hundred engineers. During his career, he worked on top-secret jobs for NASA and the military. His world leadership in the field had given him awards and recognition beyond what he ever dreamed. A driven genius, he loved his job. But while he excelled professionally, he felt lacking when it came to his love life.

He thought he would be in a relationship forever with his partner of twenty-three years—Simon Johnson. But it all ended during dinner four years ago when Simon announced he was moving to Spain and walked out the door.

Charles crashed. He still wasn't over the ordeal and doubted he ever would. But he learned to live around the pain, even though there were still times it would choke his heart until he feared it would explode.

After Simon, Charles became involved with a former subordinate, Ron Tran, who had left the company so they could be together. But last October Simon had contacted Charles for a reunion dinner. Charles told Ron about it, but not in the kindest way. But Simon never showed or bothered to get in touch again and even after many phone messages, texts, and emails, Ron never contacted him again, either.

Charles felt betrayed by Simon, yet again, and understood Ron's actions. Charles felt like he needed a new life and had decided to accept a job in Switzerland. He hoped to be settled there by the end of August.

He loved living in Clintonville, but he needed to do this. He also decided over the past several days to ask his father, Charles Wellington, II, to move with him.

They became close over the past seven months since his father had shown up at his mother's. He had— supposedly— walked out on Charles and his mother, Mary, days after Charles's birth, fifty-eight years ago. Mary and his father had different stories about his leaving, but Charles didn't care. Glad to have his father back in his life, he could never let Mary catch wind of it.

Mary had turned seventy-seven in January. For the past several years, she was the world's Senior Women's Silver Spikes Golf Championship winner and an international celebrity with her share of men. But lately she was keeping company with only one—a married movie director from France by the name of Devereux.

Charles often heard about his mother's escapades from the media or people who read the tabloids, like his secretary, Kathy. Or Mary told him about them herself. Charles didn't care to hear any of it.

Mary lived on the old Wellington Estate in Circleville, Ohio. She renovated it to be a private resort— complete with an 18-hole golf course and indoor swimming pool—where she entertained world politicians and celebrities. It all bored him.

He set his beer on the table and took the Frisbee from Sam. "Good boy." He flung the Frisbee into the yard again. His cell rang, and he picked it up from the side table. He glanced at the number and put the iPhone to his left ear.

"Hello, Father. How's sunny California today?"

"Fine, just fine, son. How are you?"

"Good. I actually had a relaxing day at home. I'm on the deck now with the boys."

"At home? All day? I figured you and Emma would be out kayaking."

"She and Stratton didn't need me tagging along. Anyway, I'm glad you called. I have something extremely important to discuss with you, and we need to set a date for us to meet."

"What is it?"

"It's a conversation we need to have in person. I think you'll be quite excited. When may I come visit?" Charles asked, his eyes drawn to the sunset over the Clintonville treetops.

"I'm busy this month because of my work schedule."

"That's fine," he grinned. His father began volunteering at a local cancer hospital after his second wife died. Charles noticed that he was more active and seemed much happier after they started spending time together. Charles had also bought him a posh condo and paid his bills, which he was happy to do.

"A date in May then. As soon as possible," Charles said.

"Hold on. Let me get my calendar."

"All right." He pictured his father hobbling through the living room to retrieve the Bridge Systems wall calendar that Charles had given him for Christmas. He wrote his daily schedule on the calendar and displayed it as if it were a Monet.

Charles took another sip of beer. *I'm sure Emma and Stratton are having a wonderful time,* he thought.

Chapter 3

"BUT YOU TOLD me you were coming home next week. Now you're telling me that you have to stay in America another month. I can't take this," Amelia whined into the phone, punctuated by her British accent. "We've been married a year and you've hardly been home."

"I know, dear, but you knew that I travel the world for my work before we married," Devereux replied.

"And you're with the golfer?"

"Yes. I'm at the hotel. I'll be going to her house soon to begin filming again."

No reply.

"Darling, you know how the tabloids are. My documentary is on Mary Wellington's life. There's no need to worry. The tabloids love a scandal. You're much too intelligent to believe anything you read in them. Besides, she's an old lady and I have the most gorgeous wife in the world," Devereux cooed.

Damn the paparazzi, anyway. It was one of the few times he and Mary had made it into the international tabloids. He had been lucky that most people he knew didn't read them. But a girlfriend of Amelia's had shown her the article. "I didn't want to ruin the surprise, but I've purchased the most beautiful gift for you. I can't wait to put it around your neck."

"You did?"

"Yes. Look forward to it. You know how I adore decorating my lovely queen with jewels."

Amelia giggled. "Okay. But you better be home in two weeks."

"I certainly will. Goodbye for now, my love."

He frowned as he ended the call and hit another icon on the face of the phone.

"*Tiens?*" a man's voice answered.

"Did he sign the contract?" They spoke in French.

"Of course. I've already deposited the money."

"Did you send the payments?" Devereux asked.

"Yes. You worry too much."

Devereux paced the grounds beside Mary's garage. He wore a robe over his pajamas and hard-soled slippers. "It's the largest investment we've received in a single payment."

"It is. But it's nothing compared to the balance of our company's assets. You were right. This is easy. Bernie Madoff will have nothing on us, and we won't get caught. What about the golfer?"

"Once we're married, I'll get her to sell this estate and start funneling her funds into an account, just like the others." He glanced across Mary's golf course.

"What about the son? Do you think he'll be a problem?"

"It's his best friend I'm concerned about. She's a former insurance fraud investigator, and she's in good with the police. I want to make sure they don't get nosy. Nonetheless, we'll be married soon. I don't want to postpone it much longer. I keep telling her my divorce isn't final because she insists on a wretched pre-nup, which we cannot have. I don't need any lawyers poking around. I can only juggle so much. Once she agrees to no pre-nup, I'll tell her my divorce is final."

The man chuckled in Devereux's ear. "You've got them mesmerized, Dev, ole boy. Do you have anyone else in line?"

"As a matter of fact, there's a very rich widow gazing into my eyes over dinners in Boston. Women are so gullible. Tell them they're beautiful, make love with them, they'll give you anything. This has been such an easy and enjoyable side occupation." He chuckled.

The man interrupted him. "Just be careful around the golfer son's friend. We don't want this one to have been a bad choice."

"I can handle it." He ended the call and slid his phone into his robe pocket. As he walked around the backyard, the sliding glass door to the patio closed. *Mary. She must have gotten up and is looking for me.*

He grew warm. He made sure he stood in his normal place along the garage where he could see around him, and he always spoke in French. No one could've been within earshot. He tightened his robe and walked to Mary's mansion, his slippers tapping on the cobblestones as he went across the patio and into the dining room.

"May I get you something, sir?"

Devereux jumped. "Oh, John. It's you. You're usually not here this early on Sundays."

"I came to bake. I don't believe Mary's up yet, is she?"

Devereux shook his head. "No, my angel is still sleeping. I believe I'll go back and join her. I went outside to make a few calls. Dreaded time differences. The reception is much better outside. Must be something about the roof here."

John raised his eyebrows. "Yes, sir. I see." He moved to the counter, opened a cupboard, and placed a glass mixing bowl on the countertop. "Breakfast will be served at eight on the sun porch."

"Thank you, John. We appreciate it. We'll see you at breakfast, then," Devereux replied, covering his mouth, faking a yawn. He turned and walked down the hallway.

John stared after Devereux. He shook his head. As he turned back toward the counter, he bumped the bowl and it fell onto the tile floor. He gasped as it shattered into glistening pieces.

Emma rolled over on the bed in the cabin that she and Stratton had rented for the weekend. She couldn't sleep and she couldn't stay in bed. She cried herself to sleep and felt like someone whipped her with a board. She did a few stretches as she stood. She needed more Advil, for sure. She had been checked out by the EMTs but refused to go to a hospital.

The Sunday morning sun streamed through the window. She walked to it and looked at the river below. It flowed low, calm, and smooth. It had crept back down into its banks overnight like a monster that had retreated to its cave.

She and the rock climbers, along with a sheriff and small rescue team, had found no sign of Stratton on the river except for his life jacket. A deputy stayed at Stratton's truck in case he returned and needed help. But he never showed.

Charles and Merek had driven five hours through the night from Clintonville, Ohio—Charles driving his Lexus SUV and

Merek following on his Harley-Davidson. Charles had slept in the other bedroom and Merek, in the living room on the couch.

Merek knocked on the bedroom door.

"Come in," she said as she sat back down on the bed. Charles came in behind Merek and sat on the other side of the bed.

The two men couldn't have been more opposite. Merek stood five-eight, buzzed brown hair, with a round European face filled with piercings on his ears, eyebrows, and lip. Right now, his hazel eyes were bleary. He wore only a pair of sweat shorts, not hiding his colorfully tattooed muscular body. It looked like a new tattoo was on the top of his foot. Emma had never seen him this uncovered. She understood why he had so many women chasing him. The man loved his ink and piercings and had the body to show them off.

Charles was the same height as Merek, but he looked dressed for a men's fashion magazine photo shoot with his long lean body, dressed in silk pajamas, robe, and slippers. His perfect salt and pepper hair matched the trimmed mustache on his chiseled face.

"I cannot believe this happened. I just can't believe it," she said.

Neither man replied. They sat on the bed in silence.

"Miss H., you go take a hot shower. You will feel better. Mr. Charles and I will cook breakfast," Merek said, rubbing her back.

She shook her head. "I can't eat."

"You do not have to eat, Miss H. You take a long shower, and it will help wash away your worry."

"Okay. I am pretty stiff," she said as she stretched and went into the bathroom.

Merek walked into the living room, ran his hands over his head, and scratched his abundantly pierced ears. He yanked up his shorts before he flopped down in a chair with Charles close behind.

"*Co za balagan*," he said.

Charles sat on the couch and glanced at Merek. "Which means?"

"What a wrecked train," Merek said.

Charles crossed his arms over his chest. "Train wreck. I concur. We need to get her away from here as quickly as possible. She'll need more pain relievers and to stay with us when we get home. This is dreadful."

"*Tak.*" Merek said.

Charles's stood and went into the kitchen. A few moments later the smell of coffee wafted through the cabin.

Merek got up from the chair, walked to the bathroom door, and placed his ear against it. The shower was on. He joined Charles in the kitchen and leaned against the counter. "We need food and pain pills for her. I will go to the gas station down the road."

Charles shook his head. "I'll go. You're on your motorcycle and I have my SUV."

Merek shrugged, went back into the living room, and stretched out on the couch. Emma came in wrapped in a towel and sat in a chair.

"Feel better, Miss H.?" Merek asked, sitting up.

She nodded. "You know what I keep thinking about?"

He shook his head.

She looked at him as if seeing him for the first time. "His life jacket swinging in that tree."

Sheriff Godfrey removed his hat and sat down in one of the cabin chairs. He placed the hat in his lap and fiddled with the brim. A younger deputy sat in the other chair. Emma and Charles sat on the couch. The thick silver chains on Merek's motorcycle boots clinked when he walked across the room and leaned against a wall, arms crossed in front of the Harley-Davidson muscle shirt tucked into his skintight leather pants.

Godfrey gave Merek a long look before he glanced at Charles sitting on the couch in a pressed starched pink oxford shirt, cuffed navy shorts, and leather loafers, no socks. He wore a chunky gold watch on his left wrist and a gold chain bracelet on his right.

It takes all kinds, the sheriff thought as he turned back to Emma.

"Ms. Haines, we would like to get Mr. Reeves's truck back to either your place or to his home in West Virginia, otherwise we'll have to charge to keep it in the impound lot over at the next town and I don't think that's necessary. We can't leave it parked in the lot at the bridge."

"I understand," she said.

"I can put my bike in the truck and drive back, Miss H.," Merek piped up.

"Okay. I'll get the key. It's in Stratton's life jacket."

She got up and went into her bedroom and brought out the life jacket. She opened the pocket and pulled out an empty key ring. She looked in the other pocket. It was empty.

"The key was here in his jacket pocket on this key ring. I know it was here. We talked about it. He showed it to me when we were on the river. I didn't want him to forget it. He left his main keys in his truck."

"It's not a problem. We can get the door unlocked and get the other keys."

"That's not the point. The key was in this pocket. I saw it."

"Yes, ma'am. I understand. The key probably just fell out."

She shook her head. "No, that key was on this key ring that's sewn into the pocket. No way could it have come off. That's why kayakers put keys on the ring sewn into the pocket, so they won't lose them." She stared at the life jacket pocket. "I don't understand this at all. If he had his key, why didn't he get his truck?"

The sheriff gave her a sad look. "I think we've talked enough this morning, Miss Haines. You've been through quite an ordeal. We'll be in touch. You get some rest." He stood, put on his hat, and adjusted his gun belt. "You're welcome to stay down here as long as you like, I understand, but it's not necessary. In fact, it might be best if you went on home. Nothing you can do down here. We'll call you as soon as we have any information."

The deputy said nothing as he followed the sheriff to the door.

"I agree," Charles said. "I believe there's a new basset hound daughter waiting for you at home and you'll both be much happier if you're together."

Murray, her former basset, had crossed over the Rainbow Bridge the past winter at thirteen. Stratton, Charles, and Merek found another lovely hound on the Ohio Basset Rescue website and she adopted Millie. She was a quiet, petite basset and Emma had fallen in love with her.

"And Maggie," Merek added.

Maggie was Stratton's golden retriever. The boys, Maggie, and Millie were all staying at Janet's—Charles's former neighbor and full-time dog sitter.

"Yes. And Maggie. They need you at home," Charles agreed.

The sheriff and the deputy said goodbye, and Merek closed the door after them.

"I'll help you get packed, Emma," Charles said.

"Are you crazy? We've got work to do."

Stratton Reeves sat in an overstuffed leather chair sipping a cold bottle of orange juice he found in the kitchen fridge. He finished reading the Sunday morning edition of *The Derby Crossing Herald* and tossed it on the side table. The front page article said he was missing after a kayaking accident, presumed drowned in a flash flood. A picture of him from a recent newspaper journalists' banquet in D.C. was in the sidebar. He found it odd that there was nothing in the paper about Emma.

Someone had cleaned him up, given medical attention to his wounds, and changed his clothes. He had on clean jeans and a red T-shirt, both a size too large. There was a large Band-Aid on his shin, and antibiotic ointment had been applied to his scratches. He sipped his juice. *At least they want to keep me alive.*

His mind raced as he looked around the stylishly decorated suite with its exposed brick walls and heavy, oak ceiling beams.

The bedroom he awakened in sat to his right, a dining area with an open kitchen to his left. Three other bedrooms surrounded the great room, behind heavy metal doors that Stratton had surmised were bulletproof. Long curtains covered thick frosted windows throughout the rooms. The faint shadows of iron bars on the other side of the shatterproof glass were testament to a security facility. He already tried to bash the windows with a chair and wasn't surprised at the result.

Tall mirrors slanting toward the middle of the room surrounded the living area above one-way mirrors, he guessed.

"Beautiful prison you have here," Stratton said to his captor, who entered the room through a heavy gray metal door that closed quickly and clicked shut behind him. A keypad was in the wall to the right of the door.

"Yes, it is. It belongs to a colleague of mine. He had it completely updated. Impeccably designed for comfort and security," the man said, gesturing around the room. He paused before he continued. "This is the guest floor. My quarters are above the mirrored floor."

"We're near Derby Crossing, Kentucky, I take it?" Stratton asked.

The man cocked his egg-shaped head. "I see you've recovered nicely. I do apologize for having to drug you, but I'm sure you understand. Just a necessity. I trust you slept well. José cleaned and bandaged some of your scrapes and changed your clothes. He said that you have a nasty cut on your shin. There's fresh clothing in the bedroom closet and drawers. I had to have José run out and get your size since you're a wee bit chunkier than Charles. And I see you've found the refreshments and food to your liking. You'll find nothing but the best of everything here."

Stratton placed the juice on the side table. "Charles? What is this about?"

The man smirked as he strolled across the white carpet and removed a pair of tight black leather gloves, theatrically, a finger at a time and tossed them on a glass-topped coffee table in front of Stratton.

He was tall and so thin his teeth looked fat in his drawn face, topped with short, gelled, bleach-blond hair. His skin looked like faded white cotton stretched over his bones. He wore an ironed blue shirt, jeans, and stylish brown dress shoes on his sockless feet.

"I had every intention of taking Charles instead of you and dealing with Emma for his ransom. But … here you are."

"How did you know we'd be in Kentucky?"

"I had a reliable source who told me that the second weekend of April, she and Charles kayak that river, where they stay, and where they park. I'm here purchasing a horse, so I thought I would deal with both matters. Save me a trip. It's a long flight from Spain. I planned to do this at some point, anyway. Everything changes, doesn't it? As they say, the best made plans. No matter. It was perfect timing."

"Who's your reliable source?"

The man gave a little snort of laughter and frowned at him, shaking his head.

"I still don't understand why you would want to kidnap me and kill Emma. I didn't realize you even knew her. Why? What's this about?"

"She obviously never told you about me." He flexed his hands and sat in the chair across from Stratton, crossing his long legs. His bony arms and fingers dangled from the arms of the chair like a stick puppet's. A large diamond ring was on his right pinkie finger. Stratton thought of a granddaddy longlegs he saw earlier that weekend, scrambling along a log.

"Well, since I'm going to kill you anyway, I'll tell you exactly why I wanted to harm your precious, little Emma.

"You see, she put me in prison because I ran into her at a very bad time and I lost my temper. I took a shot at her after I had to burn down my family home."

"She told me that an arsonist tried to shoot her, but she didn't mention any names. It was you?" Stratton asked, surprised.

Dayton Kotmister laughed. "Voila. 'Tis me," he said, palms toward the ceiling, shrugging. "All quite a shame, really. If I had the right key to the lockbox I would've never gone back to the house and run into her. I would've been on my jet without a problem. But, anyway, it's a long and complicated story. A shame I had to burn it down. The house had been in the family for generations.

"I read about it."

"Ah, yes. Rather a boring story, really. My father disowned me, and I lost all my money. Everything. Because of her. I went back to Spain as soon as I was released from prison. I discovered a very comfortable existence there. And with the help of my friends and business partners, I remade myself, so

41

to speak. But I always planned on getting even. I've always wanted her to pay both financially and emotionally. But she's dead now."

So this is the man responsible for Emma quitting Matrix and starting H.I.T.

Founded in the 1800's, Kotmister Financial and Investments became a global empire until a short time after Dayton came into the picture. Dayton was known for his obsession with horses—owning them, raising them, riding them, racing them, and betting on them—big time.

"I heard Sylvester helped spring you on a reduced sentence through his connections."

Dayton sneered. "Ah, yes. Dear, old dad. I do owe him that much, I suppose. But he cut me off, every cent, long before that. His only child. Can you imagine?" He pouted. "I had a note coming due, and that house was all I had left." He shrugged.

"You lost your ass gambling on the ponies and ran Kotmister Financial into the ground. That's why your father cut you off. But it was too late. You drained the company of all its money, and you lost all the property the company owned all over the world through your gambling payoffs. All behind your father's back. Sylvester was a good man from a good family. I interviewed him for a story. And you ruined it. Everything he and your ancestors built. You pissed it all away. That was the word on the street."

"And you would know the word on the street, wouldn't you, Mr. Award-winning-reporter?" Dayton hissed.

"Anyone who reads the papers knows it."

Dayton turned away, then back to Stratton. "No one knows the entire story. You couldn't learn that through the papers. Anyway, who would've known that she, of all people, would be the insurance investigator?"

"So you knew Emma before the claim incident?"

He shook his head. "Not directly. She was at one of my parties with Simon and Charles. I didn't have time to meet her, but I nearly fainted when I pulled up at my house and she was standing there wearing that Matrix Insurance jacket with her silly forms and a camera dangling around her neck. I regretted not running her over then, but I dearly loved that Ferrari. And she ended up destroying it anyway. I flipped it running from the police after she called them. I tried shooting her, but, obviously, I missed. I'm great at many things, but I'm a terrible shot. I hire that out. I enjoy handling other things—more of the financial nature."

"And you do that so well," Stratton said, taking a long drink of juice, eyeing Dayton with disgust. He set the bottle back on the table and leaned forward. *Should I take this crazy twig down now?*

"But I finally did run over her, didn't I? I planned on taking Charles, right in front of her. Watch her suffer. Shoot out her tires. Leave. I even hiked down the hill through the woods and watched her take your picture in front of a big rock. How sweet. I had to make sure it was you. A bit old for her, aren't you?" Dayton grinned at him before shooing his own remark away with his hand.

"Anyway, then that horrible storm blew in and you crashed into that tree." He chuckled. "I had to watch. I nearly left to go get her because I thought you drowned. You were under that tree for some time. Then you crawled out and fell back into the river when the tree broke loose."

Kotmister laughed harder. "I thought I was watching a comedy. Then you hiked up that hill, straight into my arms. That's when I decided to change my plan." He spread his arms wide and curled them around himself like a spider monkey.

"Since you were with Emma you are likely friends of Charles Wellington. I understand the two were practically inseparable." He leaned in closer to Stratton.

"I don't have to tell you anything."

"Oh, but you do, Mr. Reeves. If you haven't noticed—I'm in charge here. You and Charles are friends through her. I know it."

Stratton sniffed, raised his chin and looked at the ceiling.

"Yes, of course you are. I doubt this kayaking trip was a first date. Charles will do just as well paying ransom for you instead of her for him. It's always a pleasure to make *him* suffer. And it will be more fun this way. They won't know who it is. Money is money no matter who pays. This is quite interesting. Charles was supposed to be here, but now he'll be paying your ransom. Funny how life unfolds sometimes, isn't it?" Dayton shrugged and smirked.

"How do *you* know Charles and Simon?" Stratton asked. He waited for Dayton to continue, but he didn't offer anything further. "How do you know them?" he asked again.

Kotmister unwrapped his arms from around himself and rested them on the chair again, wiggling his long fingers as he talked. "Let's just say some of us did business together and leave it at that."

"But why now? Why after all this time? That was what, five or six years ago?"

Kotmister took a deep breath. "I need to buy a horse. And I always planned to get even with her, but it had to be fun. A game. A total surprise." He shrugged and smiled. "Life can get boring, you know?"

He leaned closer to Stratton, his stick-like elbows balanced on his bony knees. "You see, Mr. Reeves, I've found that the best way to destroy someone is through the ones they love, and they'll keep paying you at the same time. It's a win-win. Revenge with benefits. I planned to make Emma suffer both emotionally and financially. But now she's dead. Oh, well."

Stratton jumped from his chair, busted the juice bottle on the side table, and held the jagged neck toward Kotmister.

Dayton laughed. "What a mess you've made. Do sit down. Sit down. You might break a hip, old man. It's not in your best interest to make any sudden moves, Mr. Reeves." Dayton smiled up at him tapping his own chest.

Stratton glanced down. A red laser appeared on his shirt. He looked up at the mirrors surrounding the ceiling. Just as he thought—he was being watched.

"Sit down, Mr. Reeves. José will not miss."

Dayton leaned back and webbed his fingers across his chest, twirling his long thumbs. "No one crosses me and gets away with it. No one. Ever. And I always get what I want. Sooner or later. No matter what. Yes, this will work out nicely."

"What kind of insane monster are you? Is this how you remade yourself? Kidnapping and murder?"

"Money is a brutal business, Mr. Reeves. I'm sure you're aware of that."

Dayton dug a pack of Fortuna cigarettes from his breast pocket and lit one. He returned the pack to his pocket, inhaled, and blew the smoke through his bony nose.

"You live in Spain?"

Kotmister blew another long stream of smoke through a wide wicked smile. Stratton thought if snakes had teeth, they would look like Dayton Kotmister.

"Yes. I choose to be among a superior race, and it is the most beautiful country on Earth. I have an estate there that would make the most powerful men fall to their knees with jealousy. I'm rebuilding my horse collection again—the most beautiful horses in all the world. And Emma Haines nearly blew it all for me," he sneered.

"By busting you." Stratton said.

"Yes!" he screamed, then regained his composure. "But she did not ruin me. So silly, looking back."

"They have these people around called Realtors," Stratton said. "You could've sold that estate."

Dayton waved his hand in front of his face. "There was no time to sell. Don't worry about that right now. Let's stick to the point. Too many questions you reporters ask. You're no better than insurance investigators and the police. You should all mind your own business. Nothing but pests, all of you."

Dayton inhaled smoke deep into his lungs and blew it out through his nose. He held the cigarette between his thumb and index finger and studied the swirling smoke floating off its tip.

He stood and strutted across the room like a flamingo puffing on his cigarette. Dayton had to be in his fifties, trying to hold on to his thirties with his obvious face lifts and blond dye job.

The room fell silent except for Dayton walking and theatrically puffing on his cigarette.

"Why do you dislike Charles?"

Dayton blew out another long stream of smoke. "That, Mr. Reeves, is another long and complicated story that I doubt you'll live to hear."

José leaned the rifle in the corner and watched through the one-way mirrors down into the living area, listening to Dayton and Mr. Reeves through the intercom. He shook his head and turned off the speaker button. He could still see the men below him, but he grew tired of listening to them. Tired of listening to Dayton Kotmister's high-pitched voice. Tired of hearing another long and complicated story. He had heard it enough. He sat on the leather couch and pulled out the thick tattered notebook from under the end table.

After José's mother died five years ago, his priest told him that keeping a journal could be a therapeutic way to deal with his grief, and the words flowed from his pen. He felt connected to his mother through the writing. He had dozens of filled notebooks hidden in a closet at his small house in Spain, not far from where he worked at the Kotmister Estate.

He opened the notebook, flipped to the next blank page, picked up the pen from the table, and began writing, and practicing his English.

Sunday, 10 a.m., 2012 April 13: Dear Mother, I am not sure what Mr. Dayton is doing. He has kidnapped an important American journalist and run over his girlfriend. He expects me to stay here and watch this man. Shoot him if I have to. It was to be a different man. I am not sure, but I don't think Mr. Dayton had all the facts.

I know my father, so close to his father, and you said we should stay in the family business, but I am struggling. I pray to Mother Mary and she frowns upon me. But I promise to keep giving her the share of what Mr. Dayton pays me. Still, She frowns. She is sad. She shakes her head. She says it is wrong. She say, I need to go. She cries. Do you cry for me, too? Or did my father do the same for his father, too? I do not believe Dayton's father did such evil things.

But yet, I cannot leave. I cannot make the money that this man pays me and my family. I have a wife and three children. Your other son, my brother, also work for this man. It is all so complicated. We are all in it from your husband, our father. But it is so different now.

What Mr. Dayton make us do to make our money. Horrible. You invested our money in good business. Father make money. You share with charity. You, father, and Dayton's father. But his son is not like this. Your son is not like this.

Mother Mary, She cries. She shakes her head. Even though I give Her the money. She still cries. I see Her tears in my sleep. I feel them dripping on me from above my bed at night. I wake up in Her tears. I beg to Her, "I cannot make this high amount of money another way." She shakes Her head and cries. I see the Rosary shake around Her neck. The prayers I say to God, being shaken loose.

I cannot talk to Margareta. She say it is wrong, too. She want me to run. "But we make so much money," I tell her. We cannot make this money without Mr. Dayton. We want our children to grow up, have good life. Go to college. Have nice family of their own. But we must give them money to do this. I can do this. I must do this. I am the man. The provider. I make big money.

But I am so tired, Mother. And I do not want to kill anymore. I do not want to be here in this beautiful room to watch a man who does not deserve this. He is the wrong man Mr. Dayton wanted to catch. Still, Mr. Dayton say it will all work. He tell me the money I will make and I think it will buy so many good things for Margareta and your grandchildren in Spain. I cannot leave, but I am so afraid. I pray for guidance, but Mother Mary, She just cry. I do not understand.

This Mr. Stratton, he is good man. I see him on Google. He does not deserve this. Mr. Dayton, he kill his girlfriend in the black truck. But I do not understand everything. So I let Mr. Dayton tell me. I am not so smart. But I am smart to make the money for my family. I hope you and Mother Mary understand. Please understand. I have no choice.

Chapter 4

EMMA PACED THE kitchen in the cabin, talking to Joey on her iPhone. "I know Stratton's not in that river."

"That's great. He's okay then?"

"I don't know. We haven't found him yet."

"So what are you getting at?"

"Stratton's life jacket was upstream, a little ways from where he went in, at the top of that mountainside, in a tree next to the road. And where's his key? Why would he climb up the hill, take his key off the key ring, leave his life jacket, and go back down in the river and drown himself? Same thing I told the sheriff." She smacked the countertop.

"So what are you thinking?"

"I'm thinking someone picked him up. He left that jacket there for me to know he didn't drown."

A long pause. "Is there a reason he wouldn't contact you?"

"What's that supposed to mean?"

"Well, I don't know. I mean—"

"Whatever you mean, why wouldn't he contact anyone? Come on. Even if he was mad as hell at me he'd get ahold of someone and he wouldn't just take off and leave his truck and stuff here. I called his kids and Rhonda and a couple of his fishing buddies in West Virginia. No one's heard from him. Maybe he hit his head on something when he fell out of his boat and has amnesia or something. Maybe he's at someone's place and they don't know who he is. I don't know."

A tapping sound came through her iPhone speaker. She pictured Joey beating the end of a yellow pencil eraser on a yellow legal pad where he jotted notes, as usual.

"Got anything on the truck yet?" he asked.

"No. I've got Merek working on it though."

"Yeah, we've talked. I'm checking on it, too."

"Thanks. Look, Stratton's alive and I'm going to find him. I'm sending Merek back to Clintonville with Stratton's truck."

"Tell him to call me when he gets back," Joey said.

"Right. He will."

She pressed the end call icon on her phone and walked into the living room. Merek and Charles looked at her as if awaiting orders. She gave them.

"Merek, I want you to go north. I'll head south. Stop at every gas station, places like that. That truck had to fuel up someplace. Charles, you go to the cabin rental places around here. Show people Stratton's picture and ask about the truck. I still think there's a connection."

Merek stood. "Okay, Miss H."

"I think you should head back home tomorrow and take Stratton's truck. Godfrey called. They got the other keys out of it and they're bringing it over. You can probably do more there

51

than you can here. You and Joey can work together. Charles and I can take care of things down here."

"Got it Miss H.," he said before he walked out the front door. Moments later, the sound of his motorcycle roared and faded.

Charles glared at her.

"What?" she asked.

"First off, don't expect *me* to jump when you bark out your orders, *Miss H.* And you know very well what." He pointed at her.

"You really don't expect me to run home, do you? Charles, this isn't some yahoo we met on the river. This is Stratton we're talking about." She balled her hands into fists by her side.

"I understand that, but you know as well as I do that the sheriff should handle this, not us."

"If you don't want to help, then go home."

"Emma, it's not that I don't want to help, it's that I don't feel we have the resources or the authority."

She rolled her eyes. "Since when did that matter?"

"Please sit down and take a few deep breaths. I want you to think instead of react. I understand this has been a horrible experience, but you're not thinking clearly."

"Clearly? What's there to think about?" She paced the room.

"Emma, what if you find Stratton's body?"

She stopped walking and plopped down in the chair. Her shoulders dropped, and her face tightened. "He's not in that river. I know it."

"And how do you know that?"

"Because he would have his life jacket on. He climbed up that hillside and left that jacket on that tree for me to find."

"What if someone else found him and hung it there?"

"So where is he? Where's the key? If they took the key, why didn't they steal his truck? Wouldn't be hard to figure that out. Drive around and see what's parked along the river and try the key. I think he's injured and someone has him."

Charles rubbed his chin. "He hasn't any ID on him?"

"No. I had his wallet in my dry bag."

He stood and exhaled a long breath. "I'll be back as soon as I talk with the cabin owners and renters.

"Thanks." She reached out and squeezed his hand.

For the seventh time since she left the cabin, Emma checked the perimeter for signs of loose dogs before she got out of her truck and knocked on the door of another house along the road. She doubted these people would know anything either, but this is what investigations were all about—asking questions. She did this hundreds of times during her former insurance investigation career.

"What is it?" came a gruff voice from the other side of the door.

"I'm looking for a lost person and would like to speak with you."

"What's that?"

"Someone's lost. I thought you may have seen them."

"I ain't seen nobody. Go away."

She looked at the ground, kicked a rock with the toe of her Keen sandal, and shook her head. "Okay. Thank you," she yelled toward the door.

She stepped down the crumbling stone steps, making her way back to her Tacoma pickup. She got in and drove down the road a few miles to the next drive, pulled in, and sat staring at a small Cape Cod. A flock of chickens appeared from nowhere, eyeing her through her driver's side window. They strutted around the yard pecking the ground. *Maybe I should question the chickens.*

She opened the truck door, and the chickens scattered. She went up the walkway. A middle-aged woman dressed in a black sweater, ratty top, and torn black leggings opened the door before she got to it.

"If you're coming after Billy, he ain't here."

"Billy?"

"Yeah. He left over an hour ago."

"I'm not here to see Billy. My name's Emma Haines and my boyfriend's missing." She pulled her phone from her pocket and showed the woman a picture of Stratton—a close-up taken at an awards banquet two months prior in New York by a professional newspaper photographer. Stratton won first place for an Associated Press article about the European oil embargo with Iran.

The woman chuckled and shook her head. "Your boyfriend or your daddy?"

Emma gave her a look. "Boyfriend. Stratton Reeves is his name. Have you seen him?"

"No. I'd remember if I saw a man looked like that. He looks like a TV star or something."

Emma drew the phone back and stared at the picture. "Yeah. I suppose he does." She slid her phone back in her pocket.

"Do you know anyone around here that owns a huge black pickup truck?" She explained the details.

The woman laughed. "Honey, in these parts, everyone owns one of them. Why?"

"It ran over me yesterday a few miles upstream from the walking bridge that goes over the river."

"You don't look hurt much. That what happened to your face?"

Emma nodded, touching the bandage.

"You got run over by a truck and only got a scratch on your face?" The woman squinted, crossed her arms in front of her chest, and leaned back. "I reckon I can buy that. I got pushed in a well once when I was a kid, but I climbed out later. When I told my momma that my brother pushed me in the well, she said I was a liar. She said I'd still been in there if he had. I was always telling on him, sometimes making things up to get him into trouble, but this time, it was true. She still didn't believe me, though. Guess I wasn't busted up enough."

"I had on my kayak gear. It protected me. I was lucky."

"So you're a kayaker, not a rock climber? Them rock climbers are something, all right. They come down here and crawl around like little ants way up from the ground. Crazy, if you ask me."

Emma looked at her. She was a decent-looking woman who could use nicer clothes and a trip to the spa. *Like this poor gal could afford it.*

"Why'd you stop here?"

"I'm going to all the houses I see along the road. Maybe someone saw him or is helping him. Or saw that truck."

"I doubt it. Not much down here except tourists. You all look the same to us. Driving in and out of Nada Tunnel wondering where you can get a six-pack or a bottle. Tourists is funny, but they bring in money for jobs we wouldn't have no other way. I clean some of the rental cabins, round here. I'm busy all the time. Grateful for that. Can't complain. I make good money."

"Well, thank you for your time. If you think of anything or see Stratton or that truck would you call me, please? Here's my number. You can leave a message if I don't answer. Reception's not great down here." Emma handed her a business card. The woman examined it.

"Fancy. Clintonville, Ohio. Where's that?"

"About five hours north. Stratton and I came down here for a relaxing weekend. He fell in the river, went missing, and I got run over by a truck. Some weekend, huh?"

"Lordy, child. He your sugar daddy?" The woman gave Emma a crooked grin.

Emma didn't reply.

The woman looked back down at the card. "What is this—H.I.T.?"

"It's my company. It's short for Haines Insurance Training. I train insurance fraud investigators. I used to be one."

"You mean you turn in people that make bad claims on their insurance."

"Used to."

The woman frowned. "I gotta go. Good luck in finding your boyfriend."

The door slammed in Emma's face.

Merek pulled into the muddy lot of a dilapidated shack that had shown up as a gas station on his GPS. A single rusted gas pump sat listing to the left in front of the building.

He pulled off his helmet and riding gloves, placed them in the helmet, and tucked it under his arm. He rubbed his head as he walked toward the sagging screen door, gravel crunching under his biker boots. A shiny blue BMW looked out of place sitting near the building. He pulled his phone from his inside pocket and snapped a picture of the license plate—something Miss H. taught him to do long ago. He noticed a Hertz sticker on the bumper as he slid the phone back in his pocket, walked to the building, opened the screen, and closed it behind him.

The smell of burnt coffee, oil, and cigarettes hit him like a wall. Country music blared from a portable radio with aluminum foil hanging from a bent antenna. It sat on top of a lottery machine that looked like it had been there for decades. Dust covered the top of it, and a faded ink-penned sign taped across the front of it read "Broke."

The worn and cracked linoleum floor tilted to the right in the small storeroom. Nearly empty rusted racks of chips and snacks looked dusty and bewildered. A small cooler beside the door hummed and clanked, holding a few sandwiches in plastic wrap.

A woman's voice sang along with the radio, and movement came from behind a cracked glass counter. She had a beautiful voice, and Merek paused and listened. He thought of his Aunt Anka, also a beautiful singer. The singer stood and jumped at the sight of him.

"Oh! I didn't hear you. I'm so sorry. May I help you?" She held her hands over her heart, displaying long pink manicured nails.

"I am sorry. I did not mean to scare you."

Her eyes swept over him, taking in the tall handsome man with a foreign accent, holding a motorcycle helmet under his right arm, wearing a biker jacket, black leather pants, and black biker boots with silver chains. She scanned his face and ear piercings, and the colorful tattoos coiling up his neck and on the backs of his hands.

"I was listening to the radio and throwing away old cigarettes out of the case, and my mind drifted. Did you want to buy something, because, as you may have guessed, this place isn't open." She paused. "My brother will be here any second."

"I do not want to buy anything. I come here to help my friend find a big black truck that ran her over and left her for dead and to find my other friend who is missing."

She gazed at him for several seconds before she came around the front of the counter, leaned against it, and crossed her arms in front of her ample chest. She was at least a head taller than Merek and thin, radiating an air of sophistication and the chiseled beauty of a high-paid model. Her shoulder-length blunt-cut jet-black hair reflected the Florissant lighting and her makeup was soft except for the fire red lipstick, which suited her.

She wore a blue T-shirt, tight faded jeans, and stylish leather boots. Her stud earrings matched the diamond chunk on her slender wedding finger, sitting alongside a thick wedding band.

"Ran over her?"

"Yes, ma'am."

She lifted a black eyebrow.

Merek continued. "No accident. They did it on purpose, then drove away."

"That's terrible. When did this happen?"

"Yesterday."

"Is she all right?"

"Yes, she is okay. Just a scratch and she is sore."

"That's a miracle." She paused. Their eyes locked. "I'm sorry, but no. No large trucks have been by here that I know of, but then again, why would they stop? As you can see, no one's been here in a long time. There's no gas to even steal. I just came in to start cleaning out this mess. I dread the thought." She put her hands on her hips and looked around the store, frowning.

Merek followed her gaze and said, "Your singing. Your voice, it is so beautiful. It reminded me of an aunt in my homeland."

She laughed. "You think I can sing?"

"Yes. Did you take singing lessons?"

She shook her head. "No lessons. I just love to sing. I sing all the time. In fact, my husband scolds me about it." She shrugged.

They stood in silence, gazing at each other. He looked the other way when his eyes paused on the large wedding arrangement on her finger. She caught him and cleared her throat.

"This old store belonged to my parents. I played in here all the time as a kid. They worked hard to save money for my brother and me to go to college, but once I moved to New York and met my husband ..." She trailed off. "I had kids, stayed at home, and never finished. I wish I'd finished. Maybe I would've gotten a music degree, but ..." She shrugged. "Anyway, my mother died a year ago, then my father died two months ago. I came back to help take care of things. My brother will be taking over the store if he can manage it. He lives on the old family place. I left. He stayed."

"I am so sorry for your loss."

Her shoulders dropped and she smiled sadly. "Thank you."

"You are from here and now you live in New York?"

She nodded. "Manhattan. I'm just here until next week." She looked around the store again. "This place used to be one of the busiest little stores in the mountains. So many people would stop in. But I doubt he ever opens it again. It's just another one of his pipe dreams. He didn't do much of anything except sponge off Mom and Dad." Silence filled the old store. "I'm sorry. I shouldn't have ranted to you like that. So, where's your homeland?"

"Poland."

"I was there once."

"In Poland?" He lit up.

"Yes."

"Why did you go to Poland?"

"My husband had business there. I went with him. Do you live around here?"

Merek shook his head. "No, I live in Ohio. I am here to look for the truck and to find my friend, Mr. Stratton Reeves. Have you seen him?" He held out his phone and showed her Stratton's picture.

She examined it. "No. But his picture and name are familiar. Is he an actor?"

"He is a journalist."

"Ahhh. Yes, I've read his columns in the papers. He's here?"

"He went kayaking, and now he is missing. I am trying to help find him."

"Oh, no. How horrible. You've had quite a bad time. I'm sorry. Is your friend who was run over from Poland, too?"

He shook his head and removed a business card from his jacket pocket. "Here is my card with my phone. If you see Mr. Stratton or a big black monster truck with a silver grille, a GMC, please call me."

She studied the card. "Merek Polanski, Partner. H.I.T. Impressive." She asked what business H.I.T. conducted and Merek explained.

"Training insurance fraud investigators."

Interesting." She paused, outlining the card with a pink fingernail. "So, when I mentioned Poland, you lit up. Do you ever get homesick?"

Merek blinked, caught off guard by the question. "Yes."

She glanced around the old store. "I can understand that. Are your folks still over there?"

"Yes."

"Maybe you should go home for a visit."

Merek stared at her.

"Take my advice. You better go see them while you can. Time goes by quickly. I should've come back here before my father died. I didn't realize the situation. He kept it from everyone. He didn't want to burden us, I guess. I thought there was time to see him again."

The room went still except for the sound of the rattling cooler. She dropped her head, sniffled, and brushed a tear from her cheek. "Anyway, I'm sorry. I'm rambling and have taken enough of your time. Just feels good to talk to someone, you know? Anyway, maybe you should go back to Poland for a visit, I guess, is all I'm trying to say."

"Funny that you speak of that. I have been thinking about it." He paused. "Maybe you should go back and finish college. Take singing lessons. Your voice is beautiful. Time goes by quickly, as you say. Not good to waste it."

She shoved her hands in the back pockets of her jeans and shrugged. "I doubt that will ever happen. My husband would never allow it. Too late for me at this point. Anyway, I need to get back to work. It's been nice talking with you." She removed her right hand from her back pocket and held it toward him. "My name's Natalie, by the way."

Her light perfume caught his attention as he shook her hand. "Pleased to meet you. I am Merek, as on the card."

He thanked her, said goodbye, walked outside, swung his leg over the Harley, and put on his gloves and helmet.

He rode along the winding Kentucky road singing a Polish song his mother and Aunt Anka used to sing together, with New York Natalie on his mind.

It was nine Sunday evening when Charles sat down on the couch, reached for the remote, and flipped on the television. He rested his head on the back of the cushion and closed his eyes.

The three of them had split up and knocked on dozens of doors, asking people about Stratton and the black pickup. They all came up dry.

Merek came in the room in his sweat shorts and sat in the chair across from Charles.

"Do you have as much money invested in your body art as you do in your condominium and motorcycle?" Charles asked.

Merek shrugged as he watched the TV. "I do not know. I do not keep track."

Charles turned his attention back to the television for several minutes, then back to Merek." I'm taking a hot shower and retiring. I'm exhausted."

Charles handed Merek the remote and yawned. Merek flipped through the channels.

Just as Charles stood, his iPhone buzzed on the side table. He looked at the screen and frowned. It read "Unavailable." He sat back down, reached for the phone, tapped the talk icon, and put it to his left ear. "Charles Wellington."

"Mister Wellington," an odd voice came through the speaker.

"Speaking. Who's calling, please?"

"None of your concern. Just shut up and listen."

"I beg your—"

"I said listen. Mr. Reeves's life depends on it."

Charles frowned and stood.

"Whatever do you mean?"

"I mean unless you deposit eight million dollars to an off-shore account, Mr. Reeves will never kayak again."

Reeves rolled off the male caller's tongue with a slight accent. Charles looked at Merek, his eyes wide. "What? Who?"

Merek shifted in his chair, scowling at Charles.

"Just get the money. I'll contact you again with the details. I'll kill him if I don't get it. Don't let the battery on your iPhone drain. I'll be in touch." The call ended.

Charles froze. He hit the redial number. A mechanical voice told him the number didn't receive incoming calls.

"This is preposterous," he whispered.

"What is it?" Merek asked.

"Stratton's been kidnapped."

Chapter 5

Smack. Whiiiiiiiiiissssssssssssshhhh.

The golf ball sailed through the blue morning sky and dropped two feet from the hole.

"Amazing. How do you do it so consistently?"

"I'm on fire this morning, Dev. And I believe it's because you're with me. What a great way to start a Monday," Mary said. She leaned into the golf cart and gave him a deep kiss.

"Oh, I doubt that. You've won dozens of tournaments before you met me."

She smiled. "I have, haven't I?"

"Not to change the subject, darling, but did you inform Charles of our plans?"

She pulled away from him and shook her head. "No, but I intend to call him today. He's difficult to reach these days, and I'm not sure why. Perhaps he's on another one of his secret projects for work. Or maybe he's been on one of those crazy kayak trips with Emma, out of cell range. I love Emma as if she were my own daughter, but for the life of me I'll never understand their attraction to getting in those little plastic boats and going down those rivers." She shook her head at the thought. "Anyway, I've not even seen him for nearly a month. He's so secretive these days. But he is a grown man. It's hard to believe he'll soon be sixty."

"I thought you were much closer."

"We used to talk much more often, but my being with you and his job and perhaps he has another man in his life … It's all keeping us apart. I don't know. Life gets so busy. Who's to say?" She climbed in the cart, and Devereux drove them toward where the white ball gleamed like a small moon on the green. She got out of the cart, grabbed her favorite putter, and tapped the ball into the cup. She leaned over and retrieved it, tossed it in the air and caught it.

"So he's not aware of our wedding plans?"

She walked to the cart. "No. But I'll tell him everything the next time we talk. So your divorce is final, then?" she asked looking out over her golf course.

"In a few weeks, dear. Why do you keep asking?"

"After all, I mean, I want you legally single for at least a few hours before we're married."

"It's a pity we have to wait for such nonsense when I've finally found the woman of my dreams."

Mary threw her head back and laughed. "Oh, my dear, Dev. How sweet. We'll need to sign the prenuptial at some point, and we can't do that until you're officially divorced."

"If you truly loved me, there would be no prenuptial." He gave her a pouty look.

She waved a hand. "It's not me, it's my attorney. He insists. And my agent. It's merely a technicality. That's all. I've told you this. I do love you. You know that." She cupped his chin in her hand.

"Attorneys and agents. Dreadfully painful to deal with, especially your attorney. He's much too nosy. We'll be using the film company's law firm after we're married and we'll release yours."

She patted his cheek and removed her hand. "Don't be silly. Now let's get back to the house and have John fix us a pitcher of Bloody Marys and have brunch on the deck. I'm finished practicing. It's going to be a lovely day."

They rode over the plush green golf course of the Wellington Estate near Circleville, Ohio. Birds sang in the woods surrounding the property, announcing the arrival of spring. "Perhaps I won't sell this place. I can just give it to Charles. He may want to keep it. He can always rent it out while he's in Switzerland. Or Emma could live here. Or John and his wife."

"Mary, sweetheart. Charles doesn't need it, and John and his wife couldn't afford to pay the heating bill. As for Charles and Emma, that's a ludicrous idea. We agreed that it would be best to sell it. You'll be in France with me most of the time when we're not traveling." He pushed the pedal, and they sped over the last hill toward the mansion.

She stared at him. "Yes, I suppose you're right." Her voice trailed off, and she had a sudden urge to shove him out of the golf cart.

John hummed as he dusted the bookcase in Mary's library. She burst into the room in a long, silk robe and swooped over to her mahogany desk. John stopped humming.

"Good morning, John," she said, stacking and shuffling books on the desk.

"Good morning, Mary. Is there something I might help you find?" He turned and watched her. He pictured young Charles sitting at the desk working math problems and reading chemistry books instead of comic books, like most boys had read at his age. Now it was piled with novels, golf magazines, and tabloids that Mary collected. Many of them had articles about her—which she adored.

She continued to pick up books and set them aside. "I'm looking for a book for Devereux. I read it recently and I can't find it. I thought I put it here, but it appears I've misplaced it."

"I don't recall what you've been reading. I'm sorry. I've not seen much of you lately." He turned back to the bookshelves and continued dusting.

She stopped moving things on the desk and crossed her arms in front of her. "You don't care for Devereux, do you, John?"

He quit dusting but didn't turn around. He said nothing and resumed dusting.

"You won't have to worry about him for long."

John turned around. "Oh?"

"Don't sound so happy." She tightened the sash around her red satin robe. Several years ago, Charles had given her, Merek, and Emma robes for Christmas gifts that he bought while working in China. She stood as tall as her small frame allowed.

"We're getting married. I'm selling the house and moving to France. I'll give you excellent references for the new owners or for your employment file, of course. You've been with me for so long, John, I hate for our relationship to end. But Devereux thinks it's best if I sell the estate and we start new."

John's eyes widened, and he pulled the feather duster to his chest. They regarded each other for several moments.

He lowered the duster to his side. "Mary, we have known each other for a long time. May I speak openly as a friend and not as your butler?"

"Certainly."

"You're correct. I do not care for Mr. Devereux in the least and I must say, I'm shocked as to the power over you that you've given this man. You're a man's lady, and we both know you've had your share of relationships. But this man seems to have you under a spell of some kind. Frankly, it frightens me. There's just something disturbing about him."

"Thank you, John. Now, if you'll excuse me. I'll tell Devereux that you'll be serving brunch out on the patio, with a pitcher of Bloody Marys. It's a beautiful day, and I don't intend wasting it standing here listening to your gibberish."

"Have you told Charles about this?"

She raised her head defiantly. "I intend to call him today. I'll talk with him then if he has the courtesy to answer his phone when his mother calls, that is."

"I see."

"That'll be all, John."

Her robe swirled as she turned and glided out of the library and down the hall.

She put her hand on the doorknob of her bedroom and cracked open the door. Devereux's reflection appeared in the mirror across the room. He was rummaging through her jewelry box. After a moment, he held her pearl and ruby necklace up to the light from the window and rubbed the pearls. He slipped it into his jacket pocket and closed the box.

Her mouth dropped, and her heart beat in her ears. Moments passed before she gathered herself and opened the heavy oak bedroom door, walked in, and closed it gently behind her. She rested her forehead against it and closed her eyes. She opened her eyes, put on a bright face, and turned. "Darling, I can't find that book we were talking about last evening. I'm so sorry."

"Oh, that's not a problem. Sweetheart, you look so lovely."

She turned to face him. He stood in front of the dresser slightly to the side of the jewelry box. He took his right hand out of the pocket of his sports jacket and clasped his hands together.

The pocket with my necklace in it.

She stared at him, her mind whirling. His brown eyes bore a hole into her soul, as they always did. She lifted her head. "I never thought you to be a liar."

Devereux's head rose slightly as tension charged the air.

"Whatever do you mean, my dear?" he said, tilting his head like a confused puppy.

"I just got out of the shower and I've not a drop of makeup on or had a chance to put a comb to my hair." She shot him a quick smile as she walked to the dresser. "John will be serving brunch on the patio soon."

"Splendid."

"We'll go visit Charles after we eat. I've decided it would be best to break our news to him together in person."

"Ahhh, I see. Yes, perhaps that would be best. But do you think he'll be available? It seems he has no time for you these days."

Mary's neck turned red, and she didn't answer. She had been calling Charles and sending him texts and emails but received no replies. She dreaded calling his secretary, Kathy, whom Charles swore was near genius. Mary felt he kept her only as an act of sympathy. Mary considered Kathy a brainless twit.

She faced the mirror and leaned closer to her reflection. She brushed her finger over her lips and fluffed her shoulder-length silver hair. She was a handsome woman for seventy-seven, and—she knew it.

Traveling on the senior women's golf circuit for years had done her well. She took the best care of herself, physically, financially, emotionally, and—she had thought—romantically. She was a warrior who played with men until she had met Devereux while on a golf tour in France two years ago.

Fifteen years his senior, Mary Wellington did something she had never done before—fallen in love. And she intended to grasp it as quickly as possible even if it meant destroying his marriage. That wasn't her concern.

But now this. *How could he? Why would he? He's one of the largest movie producers and directors in Europe. There must be a reasonable explanation.*

She was from a poorer family and had purposely gotten pregnant. Charles's father happened to be around and was from one of the wealthier families in the area. She wanted a baby to experience motherhood—and to spite her parents at the age of nineteen. Never loving him, she married him at his insistence, but he left several days after Charles was born. She hadn't seen Charles Wellington II until he had traipsed into her house last October to talk to her and Charles. He kept babbling about telling Charles "the truth" about why he left. Mary would have none of it.

She sent him back to California with a large sum of money and strict instructions to never return or contact her or Charles again. She felt it was the least she could do, given that she lived on his family's estate and he was destitute, as far as she could tell.

She felt the warmth from Devereux's body and their eyes met in the mirror.

"You know, I wondered this morning. I know it sounds silly, but I'm just at odds as to what to wear for our wedding. Oh, don't get me wrong. I have the dress but I want to make sure my jewelry is appropriate. I don't want it to overwhelm our guests. You know, nothing too flashy. You understand. Oh, my, I must have the wedding jitters." She reached for her iPhone from the dresser top, but moved her hand to the jewelry box lid. She laughed, beginning to open it.

He placed his hand on hers and gently pushed it down. With his other hand he untied the sash of her robe as he lifted her hand from the jewelry box, kissed her fingers, and ran his fingers down the side of her hip. He leaned forward and kissed her on the neck.

"We have plenty of time to decide such things. No matter what you decide it will be perfect, my love," he whispered in her ear.

Emma, Merek, and Charles were in Sherriff Godfrey's office with two FBI agents. Agent Jay, who looked like his hair had never been near a comb, sipped his fifth cup of Monday morning coffee. Agent Robert Arnold was a handsome African-American who reminded Emma of Denzel Washington.

Charles sat in one of the two chairs in front of Godfrey's desk, wearing a pair of designer chinos, a John Varvato belt, a pink starched Ralph Lauren shirt, and Gucci loafers, no socks. He stretched his legs in front of him and crossed his ankles. He sat with his right arm across his chest, his chin propped on his left hand.

Emma walked back and forth in the small room in a light-weight flannel shirt and a pair of size-eight jeans. Her Keen sandals occasionally squeaked on the old brown tiled floor as she walked.

Merek had delayed his return trip to Clintonville due to the change in circumstances. His eyes followed Emma like a tracking device as he sat in silence at the back of the room, his arms crossing his open Harley jacket and "Born to Ride" T-shirt.

Godfrey rocked in his office chair behind a cluttered metal desk. The FBI agents stood with their arms crossed in front of the black ties peeking out of the tops of their dark suit jackets. They looked like the "Men in Black," and they made it clear when they arrived that kidnapping was their turf.

Why do they all dress like that? Emma thought as she made another turn when she came to a wall.

"The call came in on a prepaid phone. Doubt we can get anything on it," Jay said.

"Of course they called from a burner. But you can start pinging it back from Charles's phone, right?" Emma asked.

Godfrey looked at Emma. "Ms. Haines, I know you were some sort of investigator, but this is in my jurisdiction. I can understand you're upset, but we're taking all the necessary steps to find Mr. Reeves. You should consider going home."

Emma stood tall and crossed her arms in front of her.

"We've contacted our telecommunications people, Ms. Haines. We're already on it," Arnold said to Emma as smooth as Barry White, holding her gaze a second too long. He turned to Godfrey. "And this is the Federal Bureau of Investigation's matter. Not yours or Ms. Haines's."

The men glared at each other.

Agent Jay interrupted the tension, addressing Charles. "And you say the man had an accent?"

"Yes, but, as I said, I couldn't quite make it out. He could have been trying to disguise his voice," Charles answered. "At first I thought it a horrible joke."

"But *I* was with him—me," Emma said, pointing to herself again. "Not you. Why would they call you and not me? How do they know your cell number? And where's this call coming from? Reception's next to none down here in this valley. That's why we always stayed in the cabin. It's got reception and Wi-Fi."

"Mr. Reeves was likely forced to give Charles's number to the kidnapper," Jay said.

"I doubt that Stratton even knows Charles's number. Does he?" She turned to Charles.

He shrugged and shook his head. "It's unlikely. I don't re-call giving it to him or Stratton calling me on his own cell. I've talked to him. Perhaps once on my cellphone, but I believe you made the call from your phone and you handed it to him. Yes, I remember. Once while you were cooking and you handed him the phone so that I could relay additional recipe information."

"We were baking a cake for Christmas dinner to take to Mary's," Emma whispered with a sad look on her face.

"That's right," Charles said. "He couldn't read the amount of nutmeg required because he dropped something on the reci-pe card. I remember," Charles said in a low tone.

Stratton had started a food fight in the kitchen and spilled olive oil on the recipe card. Emma sneaked behind him and poured an entire cup of flour on his head. He chased her into the bedroom, where they ended up in the shower together, laughing and moving on to other activities. That was the night she asked him to move in. She raised her head, shaking off the memories of one of the best days of her life. *No time for reminiscing now.* "But why not call me or Glen or Ellen or Rhonda? Why call you?"

Glen and Ellen were Stratton's children, both surgeons in New York City.

No one answered.

Godfrey leaned back in his chair. "Let's go through it again, okay?"

"Certainly," Charles replied. He took a deep breath and straightened his spine against the chair. "Emma, please sit down. Your pacing is an extreme annoyance."

She plopped down in the chair next to him and drank the last sip of water from her bottle. She set it on the desk next to four empty coffee cups, several Pepsi and Coke cans, and more empty water bottles.

"It was nearing ten last evening, and I was sitting on the couch in the cabin watching television with Merek when my cell rang. I didn't recognize the number. It read "Unavailable." I answered as I normally answer, which is stating my name.

"A man said my name, dragging out the word Mister. I remember I thought it odd and quite rude. Then he became more offensive and told me to shut up and listen."

Godfrey nodded. "Go on."

"Well, as I mentioned, the voice sounded like a man's, middle-aged and quite snobbish with an attitude and a slight accent. Hispanic, possibly. I just couldn't tell.

"He said that unless I obtained eight million dollars to deposit in an offshore account my friend, Stratton Reeves, would never kayak again. He said to make sure my phone's battery didn't die. And he said he'd kill Stratton if he didn't get the money."

Emma looked at Charles. "The last time you said your iPhone battery. Did he specifically say iPhone?" she asked.

"Yes, he did say iPhone."

"So this guy knows your personal cell number and that you have an iPhone and not an Android. It's definitely someone who knows you," she said.

Charles looked stunned. "Why would someone I know kidnap Stratton?" He pointed to himself like being accused of something.

"Any noises in the background like a train, church bells, traffic? Anything like that?" Jay asked.

Charles shook his head. "No. Just that accent when he said Mister and Stratton's name. That's what sticks with me. I can't be certain, but as I said, slightly Hispanic, perhaps."

"Any static or other noises on the call? Was it hard to hear?"

"As a matter of fact, the call sounded a bit choppy. A little fuzzy, just for a second."

"Did you miss any of the conversation? Any pieces at all cut out?" Emma asked.

He squinted his eyes and wrinkled his brow. "No. I don't believe I missed any of the conversation."

"I keep thinking about that life jacket and missing key." She turned to Jay. "I think he was taken while he was going to his truck. It would explain why his vest was in the tree and the key wasn't there. He has it. Or the kidnapper. But why call Charles?

He was with me. And then there's his kids and Rhonda and ..." She trailed off.

"Like we told you, we've already contacted them and they've heard nothing—yet," Godfrey said.

"This will give his kids even more reason to love me," she said, rolling her eyes and raising her arms in the air and dropping them to her sides. She walked over, put both hands on the front of Godfrey's desk, and leaned toward him. "You need to get some choppers out there and look for that truck that ran over me."

"Ms. Haines. We have no choppers and few resources. I've got everyone looking for Mr. Reeves and the truck," Godfrey said, clearly frustrated.

"What about the dynamic duo?" she said turning to the agents.

"We've called a chopper, Ms. Haines," Arnold said. "We have the situation completely under control."

"Really? If you did we wouldn't be standing here, would we?"

The room buzzed with tension.

"Best if you stop fighting and work together." Merek spoke for the first time. They all glanced at him and collected themselves like scolded children.

He continued. "Maybe the kidnapper does not know or care about you, Miss H. Maybe Stratton did not tell him about his children. Or maybe the kidnapper thinks Mr. Charles has money." Merek gestured with his chin toward Charles. "Anyone out of the ordinary follow you lately?"

Charles shook his head. "No. But if they're good at tailing people, I doubt I would've noticed. I'm just not in tune to those *things*, unfortunately."

"The truck," Emma said. "I couldn't see inside that truck, all the windows were tinted so dark, even the windshield was black. I remember thinking it reminded me of Darth Vader. What if the driver of that truck had Stratton stashed somewhere? Maybe even in the truck. But then why bother trying to kill me? It's got to be connected. We've got to find that truck. It was huge. It would have to stop for gas every ten seconds. There can't be that many stations around here, right? We've got to find that truck." She punched her fist in her hand.

She walked around in another small circle then stopped. "Oh, no."

"What is it?" Arnold asked. Everyone's eyes were on her.

"It's Calhoon. It's Earl Calhoon. He's got Stratton."

The chains on Merek's boots clanked as he dropped his feet to the floor and sat up. "You think, Miss H.?"

"It certainly was not Earl Calhoon who called me," Charles said.

"He just had someone else make the call for him. Stratton worried about Calhoon coming after me. I should've listened." She sat down in the chair and dropped her head in her hands. She rubbed her face and looked up.

"Calhoon?" Arnold asked. "The character you helped lock up in West Virginia? Read something about it doing your background check." He cleared his throat and straightened his tie.

She gave him a long look before she explained the entire story with the help of Charles and Merek.

Godfrey's phone rang, stopping the discussion. He picked up the receiver and had a short conversation of a few grunts and a couple of yeses before he hung up.

"That was the sheriff two counties over. Hikers found a black pickup burnt to a crisp along the woods. Matches the description of yours. Several gas cans in the back. VIN's been popped out, and no sticker on the inside door. You want to take a ride and check it out?" he said, looking at Emma with weary eyes.

"You bet I do."

Emma jumped out of the back of the cruiser before it came to a stop alongside the gravel road. She ran toward the yellow police tape. The FBI agents pulled in behind them in a black Mercury sedan.

Emma, Godfrey, and the agents stood along the edge of the scene, peering toward the truck. Several men in white scrubs, booties, and rubber gloves swarmed around like bees near a black evidence vehicle. Two of the men had cameras hanging from their necks.

The air smelled like a steel mill, burning rubber, and gasoline. The truck sat on melted tires on an old farming road that ran along the edge of a woods.

"That's probably it," she said, thinking of a stolen car ring case she and Joey had worked on together. They found not only a car, but also a burnt corpse inside. Her heart jerked.

An older man dressed in a black sheriff's uniform limped through the field of corn stubble and over to them.

"What did you find?" Emma asked.

The old sheriff shook his head. "Nothing much in the truck. Won't be a print or much evidence of anyone in there after that. They'll go over it with a fine-toothed comb, though. There is another set of tire tracks, likely followed the truck in here parked alongside it on the passenger side. Two sets of footprints. Looks like some drag marks, then a horseshoe shape of fooprints spaced about five feet apart, facing each other, like two people were carrying something between them. Then more commotion on the passenger side of the vehicle."

"Stratton," Emma whispered.

The old sheriff eyed her. "You the girlfriend, I take it?"

"Yes. What kind of tire tracks on the other vehicle?" she asked.

"Probably a car, normal tread, nothing wide and fancy or big like those truck tires. That thing was built to run over cars at a show or something. Anyway, we'll try to get casts made before the weather lets loose again. My men are going through the edge of the woods and the surrounding cornfield. May find something. More storms moving in." He looked at the graying sky before he turned back to Emma. "We'll take all the normal precautions, let ya know what we find. Evidence guys are all over it."

"My office checked again, but still no stolen vehicles reported in the state matching the truck description," Godfrey said.

"No reports across the country of a stolen truck like this that we can find, either. Must've been purchased and modified," Jay piped up.

Emma thanked the sheriff and walked away. Agent Arnold came up beside her and cleared his throat. "Miss Haines, I'm sorry about Mr. Reeves. If there's anything I can do to help you …" He trailed off, looking embarrassed. "I'm sorry. I just meant. Never mind." He turned away.

A spark of electricity had flown between them when he walked into Godfrey's office. Had it been another time, another place, and certainly other circumstances, she might have enjoyed a dinner and maybe more with him. She gave him a lopsided smile and a nod. "Thanks. Appreciate it. Sorry I've been so nasty. I know you're just doing your job."

He turned away, shoving his hands deeper into his suit pockets. His phone buzzed. He reached for it and strolled away from Emma. She followed a few paces behind. At least she and Merek and Charles were finding the same information. Nothing. They called every car dealer and tinting company around the area, but Merek and Charles were checking again back at the cabin and Joey was hitting the database for her.

Arnold turned toward her. She stood and looked at him.

"Communications department on the phone. They have nothing further to report. I'm sorry."

"Me, too," she said, looking out over a cornfield. "Me, too."

Chapter 6

CHARLES SAT ON the couch flipping through the *WSJ Magazine* that had been in his suitcase. He tossed it aside, stood, and walked around the room. He owned nearly everything in that magazine, and it wasn't doing any good looking at more to buy. *How much is enough?*

He thought a great deal about the situation and another wave of guilt hit him. *I should've gone with Emma and Stratton. Then maybe this would not have happened.*

Stratton loved Emma. Charles could see it in his eyes when he looked at her. This made Charles both happy and sad. Since Stratton and Emma had met, he and Emma had spent little time together. *But if she hadn't met him, would I be spending so much time with my father?*

He walked out the door and stood on the deck overlooking a small creek that fed into a fishing pond below the cabin.

He thought of salmon fishing. He never fished, but the pictures in papers and reading the adventures about it put it on his list of things to do. He would take his father. *Yes, we'll fish in Switzerland and Alaska and rivers beyond. Maybe I'll teach him to kayak.*

He smiled. "Yes, I'll take my father kayaking on a beautiful lake in a tandem. He'll love it."

He couldn't stray far from the cabin, but he needed fresh air. He trotted down the steps toward the gravel path leading to the pond. He walked down the drive and stood along the bank. He checked his phone. Plenty of reception. He put his phone back in his pocket, picked up a rock beside his foot, and threw it into the water, shattering his reflection.

He turned and looked at the cabin on the hill that he and Emma had rented on this weekend for years. Memories rushed over him. Now, Emma and Stratton would likely rent it. Or not.

Emma stood in the kitchen of the cabin and poured a fresh cup of coffee into a mug. She didn't want to sleep. She didn't want to dream.

She sipped the strong liquid and leaned back on the counter. Her heartbeat increased, and she closed her eyes. "I'm sorry, baby," she whispered. She wiped a tear from her cheek.

She looked out the window as evening moved in. She set the mug on the counter and leaned toward the window, looking right and left. She wanted to see an owl looking at her with those wild wise yellow eyes. She wanted the owl to tell her the answers, whether she liked them or not.

Who? Who? Who? Where? Where? There. There.

She wanted to find him, take him home, then tell him to leave her alone. She was nothing but trouble. That was obvious.

The only job she knew how to do often dropped a net over her and the people she loved. But sometimes law enforcement was like that. You did your job—no matter what.

But Charles was right. She wasn't an investigator anymore, but a consultant. She needed to stop chasing bad guys. Let the police and sheriffs and the FBI handle things without her butting in.

"After I find Stratton, I will," she said aloud.

She pulled back from the window, picked up the mug, and stared down at the black steaming coffee.

Charles walked into the kitchen wearing his red silk pajamas and slippers. He pulled a glass from the cupboard, poured himself a cup of tomato juice from the refrigerator, took it to the kitchen table, and sat down. He pulled his iPhone from his pocket and placed it on the table.

"It's eight thirty. Jammies already?" she asked.

"I'm planning on retiring early. Merek snores. Loudly. I was awakened twice during the night." He yawned and ran his fingers through his graying hair.

She remembered when Charles's hair wasn't gray and she colored hers less often. They met each other on the Olentangy Bike Path seventeen years ago, both of them riding to work in opposite directions.

She introduced Charles to kayaking, and he loved it as much as she did. She tried not to think of him moving to Switzerland.

"Merek headed back to Clintonville. He can do more for us there than here. "

"Good. At least I won't have to hear him snore."

She drank her coffee.

He drank his juice.

"I don't think it's Calhoon," she said.

Charles glanced at her and took another sip of juice. "You were certain of it earlier. Why the change?"

"Calhoon isn't the type to know anyone who knows anything about offshore accounts."

"But we don't know who he could've hooked up with since his escape. Perhaps someone more educated and well-to-do and he's forcing them, putting them up to making the calls, as you mentioned."

"How would Calhoon get your cell number? Stratton doesn't know it. Your number's not in his contact list on his phone. I checked. He left it in my truck. I went through it last night and sent the list of contacts to Godfrey. And to Joey. I seriously doubt Stratton knows my number, or even his own, for that matter. I don't think it's Calhoon."

A heavy silence hung in the air.

"I need to call Janet about the boys, but I'm exhausted. Could you inquire about them when you check up on Millie? Just ask how they're doing, and tell her I'll be home as quickly as possible."

Emma didn't reply.

"You know we're on the suspect list, too. I'm likely at the top—spouses, partners, friends, even distant acquaintances—always get considered first. And the FBI has already checked us out, probably figuring that you, Merek, and I didn't cook this up."

Charles raised an eyebrow. "We have nothing to hide and we're certainly not involved in this horrid affair, other than being victims."

They sat in silence for some time until Emma said, "Simon went to Spain."

His eyes held hers. "The thought of someone with a slight Hispanic accent and Simon hasn't crossed your mind?"

"Certainly not. That wasn't Simon on the phone. Simon Johnson would never kidnap Stratton or anyone else. That's ludicrous. He doesn't even know Stratton. And he certainly doesn't need the money."

"At least you don't think he does. And what if he's been tailing all of us? He was in Clintonville in October. He called me, and then he called you. And he never showed or tried to contact us since. Don't you think that's weird? He certainly knows your cell and he used an untraceable phone then. He could be using another one now."

Charles closed his eyes and shook his head. "That's ridiculous, Emma."

She took a long drink of her coffee. "Maybe you should just ask the kidnapper if he knows Simon. See what he says—"

"What? I just told you, Simon would never be involved in such a horrific situation. He … he … has no motive. And I know his voice. It's NOT him. It's NOT Simon!"

"Then ask the kidnapper why he called you and not me. Or something like that. I don't know. If it's Simon—"

"It's NOT Simon."

"Charles, stop protecting him. Whoever it is knows your cell number, and you said the man may have been trying to disguise his voice and has a *slight* accent. Simon could've picked one up in three years."

"But not in a few months. He had no accent when I talked to him in October. Did he when you talked to him?"

"I honestly don't remember. I was yelling at him the entire time for calling me and not you. Maybe he's faking it. Maybe he's in it with someone else. Maybe he's putting someone else up to it. We don't know who he's hooked up with, either."

"Emma, Simon may be a lot of things, but he is NOT a kidnapper or would be one to fake an accent." He held his left hand with his right, trying to hide his twitching left pinkie, but she noticed.

"I'm not sure——." The ringing of his iPhone on the table interrupted him. He looked at the screen, nodded, picked up the phone, slid his right index finger across the face of it, hit the speaker icon, and held it out near his ear.

"Do you have the money, Charles?" the man's voice came through the speaker. Charles stood and walked in front of Emma holding the phone out between them.

They froze.

"No."

Pause.

"Why not?"

"Where do you propose I retrieve that amount of funds?"

The caller laughed. "If you don't have it I'm sure the authorities can get it quickly."

Charles took another long pause, as he had been instructed to do, inhaled, and looked at the ceiling.

"Talk or I will hang up and kill Mr. Reeves." There. The Hispanic accent.

Charles's eyes flicked to Emma's. They both nodded. He paused as long as he dared. "I'll not get you a cent until I know that Mr. Reeves is safe and unharmed. I demand to speak with him or get proof he's alive and well and is not being mistreated. I demand his release and that we put an end to this nonsense and Mr. Reeves is returned immediately, unharmed." He and Emma locked eyes. "Who are you, and how did you get this number?"

"Mr. Reeves is quite comfortable." The man chuckled.

"Who are you? Why are you calling me? Why not call—"

"So many worthless questions. I'm calling you because you are Mr. Reeves's closest contact here now that Emma Haines is dead."

The color drained from their faces.

"She's what?"

"Dead. I ran over her. It was not my original plan, but it was even a more wonderful feeling having the famous Mr. Stratton Reeves with me to see her dead in the road like vermin. It was supposed to be you I would call her about, but you didn't come with her as you normally do. But her boyfriend will do just fine."

Charles gasped. Emma's eyes grew wide.

"She's—"

"Dead. Enough nonsense. I have to go. I'll contact you one more time and tell you how to deposit the money. We've wasted too much time. No more delays."

The call went dead.

"I knew it! I knew it! He was driving that truck! And it's someone that knows us. That's for sure. I caught the accent, but other than that, I have no idea. You?" Emma asked.

Charles shook his head. "Absolutely no clue."

There was a sharp knock on the front door. She ran to it, eyed Agent Arnold through the peephole, unlocked it, removed the chain, and opened the door.

"We got everything recorded and can probably get a general location on the phone."

"I knew it!" She pointed a finger in Arnold's face.

He grabbed her finger and lowered her hand. "Yes, Ms. Haines, you were correct. But you need to calm down. You're too close to this. You just need to calm down and back off. Let me and my people handle it. You have no jurisdiction to be involved. You need to go home."

Emma glared into his large brown eyes. "I'm sure you scrubbed the call?"

"Yes."

"And?"

He looked at her for a long moment. "We heard what sounds like a horse whinnying in the background."

"A horse?"

"A horse."

"So this guy's around here on a horse farm?"

"Could be."

"Another burner. Different carrier."

"Likely." Arnold sat down in the chair beside Charles, who still sat motionless staring at the phone, the color drained from his face. "You okay?"

"This just can't be happening," Charles said.

"I'm gonna get this guy and nail him to the wall," she yelled, walking around the room, punching her fist into her hand.

Arnold left Charles and walked to Emma. "Miss Haines, your investigative background and Mr. Wellington's security clearances with every government on the planet are respectable, to say the least. But *you* need to stay completely out of this investigation. Do you understand?"

She crossed her arms in front of her and gave him a look.

He put his hands on his hips and looked away from her then back. "It's clear now that the caller had planned on dealing with you and kidnapping Charles. He said his plans had changed. That's why he's calling Mr. Wellington. He thinks you're dead."

"And we need to keep it that way," she said.

Arnold's cell buzzed. He listened. "Got it." He ended the call.

"Where?" she asked.

He sighed and dropped his shaking head before he looked back at Emma.

"Pinged off a tower outside Derby Crossing."

"I'm sorry, Mother. I've been caught up in this horrid case. I have to stay off of my cell. I've purchased a second for personal calls."

"You could've at least given me your new number and explained to me what's going on. You need to keep out of this, Charles. You could be killed."

"I don't believe I can keep out of it since the kidnapper is calling me. I can't discuss it with anyone. Let's talk about you. How have you been?"

"Like you care."

"Mother, please. Stop being dramatic."

"I'm not being *dramatic*. I need to discuss an important matter with you immediately. When can you meet me?"

Charles sat on the couch, holding the cell to his ear with his left hand. He fell back into the cushions.

"I cannot leave until Stratton is found. Whatever it is, it will most certainly have to wait. Stratton's life is the most important issue at hand. You do realize that, don't you?"

"Yes, but this is important, too, Charles. It concerns your future."

Charles sat up. "My future?"

"Charles, I need to discuss something with you."

"Mother, I need to stay close to my phone and in Kentucky and do what the authorities instruct. And I still have to work. I have a large project that's coming to a close. It's not a good time."

"You need to leave this alone, Charles. You're my only son. You could get hurt or even killed."

"I'm well aware of that, Mother."

"Oh, what's the use trying to talk with you?" she snarled. "I need you here, now! This is no way to treat your mother. Call me when you get home."

The call went dead.

Charles placed his new cellphone on the table, picked up the phone the kidnapper had been calling, and stood. He was in no mood for one of Mary's tantrums. He walked into the bathroom and set the iPhone on the countertop. He looked at himself in the mirror. His eyes were hollow, and red moons hung below his pupils. "I look *hideous*," he said.

His skin looked like putty. He hadn't slept well since Stratton's kidnapping or looked this ragged since … He didn't even want to start thinking about that, but it had already been resurrected.

All afternoon he had to discuss Simon and see Simon's name outlined in a red box with a green line going to Dayton Kotmister's name on that whiteboard.

He took off his clothes, folded them, placed them on the toilet lid, put on the shower, and stepped in. The hot water pelted his muscles. He turned in slow circles, rubbing his arms, his chest, and his head.

Mary was right. This was a dangerous situation, and he was caught in the middle of it. He knew danger. He faced it several times on his job working overseas in various countries, but he was always shielded from it. And it wasn't danger like this. This was different. This was personal. Very personal—beginning with Emma and branching out like a web they were all caught in. *Or does it begin with me and branch out snaring Emma and Stratton?*

He closed his eyes and kept turning under the hot water, thoughts clattering in his head like marbles rolling down a tin roof.

He turned off the shower and stepped out. As he reached for a towel, the cell buzzed alerting him of a text.

Chapter 7

"Do you realize that I switched nights with Lightning to get tonight off just so I could go riding with you? The two-for-Tuesday night tips I would've gotten were going to pay for my new dress I was going to buy for our trip next weekend. How thoughtless of you! Why are you canceling our date? There's nothing you can do about Emma's boyfriend tonight."

The evening before, Emma and Charles had left for Derby Crossing and Merek had hauled his Harley back to Clintonville in the back of Stratton's truck. After he dropped the truck off at Emma's, he came home and called Joey. They were working together to try to find information to send to Emma. He got little sleep.

He sat at his granite kitchen counter, sipping coffee and glancing through the Tuesday morning paper while holding his phone away from his ear. He set the phone on the counter, hit the speaker button, and stared out the glass wall of his high-rise condo at the Olentangy River. The water glistened in the sun like black sequins.

His mind flashed back to Ludnella Czerwinski, the woman who always wore sequined tops and the woman he most nearly fell in love with and who almost talked him into moving to Colorado with her. His memories were interrupted by Fantasy's shrill voice.

"Are you still there? Are you even listening to me?" she squealed.

"You will not need to buy a new dress for any trip with me now or ever." He hit the end icon on his Samsung and threw it across the room—another time the protective case came in handy.

"I need a holiday—alone," he muttered as he walked over to retrieve the phone.

The phone buzzed in his hand. "*Ah, Gowno!*" He frowned, shook his head, and hit the accept call icon.

"Yes, Mr. Nelson."

"Merek, I realize that Emma's boyfriend has been kidnapped. She called and explained the situation and I saw it mentioned on the news, but I still have adjusters to train and a business to run. I had to cancel this training—again."

"We apologize, but she will not be able to work until Mr. Stratton is found."

A long silence came from the other end of the line. Merek, and everyone else, knew that Calvin Nelson had the major hots for Emma and could not care less that Stratton Reeves had been kidnapped. In fact, Merek had a quick thought that Calvin Nelson could be behind the kidnapping. He mentioned this to Agent Arnold before he left Kentucky and had felt good when Calvin's name went on the whiteboard. Emma had to explain the relationship between H.I.T. and Calvin Nelson—and Calvin's obvious admiration for her. Merek smiled at the thought of him being investigated.

"So who will be available? Should I hire another vendor while she's out?" he bellowed into Merek's ear.

"I would be glad to lead the class."

Calvin snorted. "You've got to be kidding. Nothing personal, but you just don't have what it takes, *Merek*. You're not the type."

Merek made a nasty face toward the phone but kept silent. Matrix Insurance was their largest client, and he knew Emma wanted to keep it that way—at least for now. Emma was loyal to Mr. Matrix, the elderly founder and CEO of Matrix Insurance. Unfortunately, Calvin came with Matrix.

Merek faked a laugh. "You are right, sir. Is there someone there that can help?"

A long silence and then Calvin said, "Yes, I suppose. Email me the presentation with the changes I sent you yesterday, and I'll find someone here for now. But if she's not back soon, I'll have to find another vendor."

Merek knew he wouldn't let Emma go that easily, especially if he thought Stratton was out of the picture.

"Yes, Mr. Nelson. I understand. I will make the changes, send it, and relay your message to Miss H. Thank you for being understanding in this situation. I gotta scram."

He ended the call, walked to the kitchen, and poured his second cup of coffee. Perhaps he would ride his bike to Matrix and throw his laptop at Calvin Nelson before he rode to the strip bar to throw something at Fantasy besides fifty-dollar bills.

Oh, Ludnella.

Calvin Nelson dropped his office phone receiver onto the cradle and hit the intercom for his secretary.

"Yes, Mr. Nelson?"

"Get Emma Haines on the line. I don't care how many times you have to call her. I need to talk to her. Now."

"But—"

"No buts. Now!"

He punched the button and leaned back in his chair, propping his scuffed size thirteen shoes on his desk. He could barely see his toes over his paunch. He would have his new secretary, what's-her-name, take them to the shoe shiner down the street later. He frowned. "Secretaries. Not any of them have the work ethic to stay here for more than a month," he muttered to himself.

He rocked in his chair, his head resting in his intertwined fingers. He scratched his head. His new hair plugs bothered him, but it didn't matter. Stratton Reeves had a full thick head of gray hair and soon—so would he.

He leaned forward and Googled Stratton Reeves on his MacBook. Several articles popped up about his disappearance including one in *The New York Times* and one in *The Washington Post.* They would, his being a famous journalist. Calvin leaned in for a better look at a picture of the smiling Stratton Reeves receiving a writing award last summer. He snickered.

"So, Mr. Reeves. You're gone, and I'm still here with Emma. What a lovely coincidence. Thank you for saving me the trouble of having to get rid of you, you old geezer."

He laughed and clicked on a bookmark in his Favorites. Emma's website appeared. He clicked on her bio page and leaned in closer to her picture, his nose nearly touching his monitor.

"You and I will be married soon. You'll see. You'll want me more than anything. I'll make it happen." His thoughts were interrupted by the intercom buzzer.

"Mr. Nelson, Miss Haines is on line one."

He punched line one.

"Emma, is there any news on Stratton? I'm so sorry this has happened."

A pause and a sigh before she spoke. "I can't give your presentation to the new investigators, Calvin, I'm sorry. I have to stay in Kentucky."

"Don't worry about that. Merek is sending me the updates, and I'll have someone here do it. I may even break down and do it myself. Don't you worry about a thing. You're under so much stress right now, Emma. When you come home, I'll take you to a nice dinner."

"I really can't talk right now. I need to keep off my cell."

"Do you think they'll find him?"

"Yes. We'll find him."

Calvin Nelson leaned toward his monitor.

"I'm glad you're so certain. Listen, if there's anything I can do to help. Anything at all."

She didn't answer.

"If there's anything, you just let me know."

"I'll have Merek let you know what's happening."

"I appreciate that, Emma. I'm quite concerned. You need to make sure you take care of yourself."

"I am. Goodbye."

"Goodbye."

He set the phone in the cradle. "He won't be back, and you'll come running to me."

Someone knocked hard on the outside door and yelled several times, but Stratton couldn't make out what they were saying. He ran to the door and put his ear against it. A woman.

"Help. Help. I've been kidnapped. Call the police. Call the police," he answered, pounding on the door.

The pounding and yelling stopped. He put his ear against it again, and the pounding and yelling resumed. The woman yelled in Spanish.

"Mr. Reeves, do get away from the door." Dayton said, sipping coffee as he ambled through the gray metal door and sat down at the kitchen table. "No one will ever find you here."

Stratton lowered his head and slowly shook it from side to side. He turned to Dayton. "And exactly where is here?" he asked, fully not expecting an answer. He trudged back to the kitchen table and sat down in a chair across from Dayton.

Dayton took another sip of his coffee, eyeing Stratton over the rim of his cup. He set the cup down, folded his fingers, and placed his hands on the table.

"Oh, let's see now." He leaned back, tapping his chin with his right index finger. "I tell you where you are, you attack me, steal my cell, and make the rescue call. Whooooo. I'm shaking." He shook his hands in front of Stratton's face as if he were afraid.

"How disappointing. I expect more than that from you. You're well aware that if you as much as come toward me— you'll be dead. And I never carry my cellphone when I visit you. I leave it upstairs in my quarters. In a safe.

"And that door there," Dayton pointed with a long manicured finger, "is just the first door to the hallway that leads to a second door with a different code. You'd be trapped like a rat in a box even if you made it through that door."

Stratton's hopes fell again. Another block in his plan to attack Dayton when he came into the room, use him as a shield, and bid with José.

"Besides, it was one of my people at the door anyway."

"Banging and yelling like that?"

Dayton shrugged. *I'll deal with Margareta later.* He told her not to come to talk to her husband, José, but she didn't listen.

"Anyway, I sent a text to Charles last night and the money went immediately to my account. I would've loved to have seen the look on his face."

Stratton looked away. "This is all a game to you, isn't it?"

"Life is a game, Mr. Reeves. Now, if you'll excuse me, I have things to attend to. Then I'm off for home."

"And me?"

Dayton glanced up at the glass mirrors.

"It's that easy? Shooting a fish in a barrel for you? Cold-blooded murder?" Stratton said, standing and glaring Dayton in the eye.

"Mr. Reeves, you're of no use to me. I'm sorry. You can do me no good. I thought about it, but I haven't the time or the desire to keep you. I want to go home as soon as my horse deal is closed."

"Why didn't you just have one of your goons come over here and buy the horse for you? Why do this yourself?"

"Because there are two things that are personal to me. Horses and revenge. I do those things myself."

"But the killing? The dirty work? You hire that out. Except for Emma. Is that right?" Stratton glanced at the mirrors.

"Enough of this talk, Mr. Reeves. It annoys me. As I said, I have no need to keep you around and I, certainly, can't let you go."

"But maybe you do have a need for me."

Dayton laughed. "And why would I need you? I call your family for more ransom? Boring. And too complicated. Charles can make monthly installments on you. What he is paying now is only a deposit. Technically, this project is over. I have no reason to keep you around. No one will ever know if you're dead or alive. They'll keep paying me out of sheer hope for your return."

A project. That's what this is to him—killing Emma—part of a project? Stratton inhaled deeply and exhaled. "What if I write your life story? Your legacy."

Dayton laughed loudly like a sick clown for several seconds before he abruptly stopped. "Now, wait. That is a thought. My life story." He looked off as if he were watching a ship pass along a horizon. "Written by you, my good friend—the famous journalist Stratton Reeves. It would likely sell more than anyone else's boring biography."

"With my name on the book, it will probably be a best-seller. And you can have the proceeds to help buy horses. Build your own racetrack. You could have your name on many things, along with the story of your life, all around the world," Stratton said.

Dayton's eyes twinkled as he stood and slowly strode around the room. "I'll tell you what. I'll think about it." He turned and looked up toward the mirrors. "Don't shoot him just yet, José. I'll be back later. We'll decide what to do then."

He left the room, coffee cup in hand, through the metal door. Stratton flinched at the click of the latch.

He looked up at the mirrored walls surrounding him. "How about you? Anything you want to put in this book, José?"

Dayton sat alone on the patio of the only Spanish restaurant about forty miles from Derby Crossing. He ordered in fluent Spanish. Poncio, the young waiter, wanted to chat in his native language, but Dayton made it clear he had no interest.

As he ate, he thought of his hidden estate in the mountains of Spain. He missed his Olympic-size pool and his sauna. Soon there would be more horses. And he would own another horse of his dreams—King's Runner.

As luck would have it, a friend of Dayton's was a descendant of the founder of the Spanish mafia and owned the horse farm outside Derby Crossing. Dayton had stayed there years ago. When he called and told his friend he needed a discreet place to stay, the owner told him he could use the ranch as long as he wanted. He was staying at one of his other villas and wouldn't be there for months.

It was perfect, offering extreme beauty, horses to ride, comfort, and security, hidden deep in the Kentucky mountains. The staff lived on the other side of the property—far enough from the main house that they didn't see the comings and goings.

He sent José to work out the details about the horse several weeks ago. While Dayton had planned his trip to Kentucky, he noticed the Red River wasn't far from the ranch and recalled Simon telling him about Emma and Charles going on their annual kayaking trip. And that's when he crafted his plan. The horse would be paid for easily—along with sweet revenge. He called José and told him what to do.

Before Dayton's arrival, José paid cash for a black Toyota Camry, a black Honda Accord, and the huge black truck. He found them for sale in yards in the hills of Kentucky. When José saw the brand new truck, he had to have it. The seller had lost his job the week before. José had been the angel at the door with a wad of $30,000 in cash and no questions or title needed. He knew Dayton would like the truck, too. And he did.

José had the windows tinted on the truck for Dayton's arrival and their trip to the Red River. He filled the dual tanks and placed additional tanks of gas in the truck bed so they wouldn't need to stop and refuel at a station.

Dayton arrived in Kentucky in a private jet, which landed at the small airstrip on the ranch. After Dayton had nabbed Stratton, he met José at the road beside the field two counties away. José was experienced at finding out-of-the-way places.

They moved a dead-weight sleeping Stratton into the Camry before José torched the truck and they returned to the ranch. That evening, they slammed through three bottles of Spanish wine to celebrate while Stratton slept off the knockout drug.

Dayton planned to have José kill Stratton soon, but the thought of having a book written about his life by an award-winning journalist kept nagging him.

Poncio returned with more water and the check.

"Would you like anything else, *Señor?*" Poncio asked in Spanish.

"No. Go away and leave me alone," Dayton snapped back in Spanish.

Poncio retreated annoyed, hurt, and confused, wondering what he did to upset the rude man who never took off his sunglasses and hat on such a cloudy day.

Dayton took out his iPad and opened the *El País* newspaper. He read for several minutes before he pulled his iPhone from his pocket, tapped an icon, and held it to his ear.

"Sí?"

"I will be bringing a guest back with me to stay indefinitely. He'll need to be under constant surveillance. I'll let you know when to send the plane. Don't try to contact me. And tell that crazy sister-in-law of yours that she better do as I say or she won't be around to have a choice. She pounded on the door earlier, trying to talk to José. I imagine they're quarreling again and he won't talk to her. But their affairs cannot disturb my plans. Or my guest. Do you understand?"

"*Sí.*"

"I'll have a talk with her myself, but I suggest you make it quite clear to her not to ever go against my wishes again. Ever!" He hit the end button on the face of the phone and slid it into his jacket pocket.

He ate his meal and gathered up his iPad. He placed cash, including a forty percent tip, in the restaurant binder and dropped his napkin on the table beside his plate. He stood, drained the last sip of wine from his third glass, and placed it on the table. He strode quickly out of the restaurant, got into the Camry, pulled out of the parking lot, and headed back to the horse farm.

I will let him write my story, then I will have José's brother kill him.

José listened as Stratton rested between doing sit-ups. "Do you want a chapter in this book, too? Let me ask you a question, José. Why do you work for this man? He's a murderer. Nothing but a common criminal. And he's dragging you and your family down with him."

José placed his forehead against the wall and pushed the talk button on the intercom. "*Señor* Kotmister and my family, we go back long time. My father worked for his father."

Stratton shook his head. "A family affair. Sylvester was a good man, not a kidnapper or a murderer. He worked honestly and hard. So your father must've been a good man."

"*Sí.*"

"So what happened? What went wrong with Dayton? Why are you doing this? The money? Do you like this kind of life? Is it worth it? José, you'll surely be caught and sent to prison for kidnapping. And if you kill me you'll be a murderer, too. Just like Kotmister. He murdered the woman I loved." The last words caught in his throat. "You'll never get out of prison. Or worse."

"Mr. Kotmister make sure we do not get caught. We watch each other's back."

Stratton laughed. "The only thing Dayton Kotmister watches is his money and his horses. I doubt he cares anything about you or anyone else. Do you think he'll take any of the heat for you when you get caught?"

José didn't answer.

"José, I can pay you any amount of money you want to let me go and walk out of here right now. No questions. Nothing. I won't come after you. You set up an account and tell me where to send the money. That's it. That's all. You have my word. I'm not asking you to kill anyone or kidnap anyone. You could come out a hero in this if you play your cards right. Instead of spending your life in prison or worse. Think about it. What's your price? If I write this book you could be the hero in it, not Dayton. I wouldn't use your name, but you know you would be the hero. He's putting you up to all this. Or this could be your time to tell your story, José. The story of your father and setting things straight."

"I do not have the code to the doors, Mr. Reeves. I cannot let you go."

Stratton's fists curled. *Damn Kotmister.* "But we can make a plan so that when Dayton comes back in here, you can come in behind him, block the doors open, and help me take him. It won't be hard, José. We'll tie him up and I'll take him with me."

"No, *Señor. Señor Kotmister* would kill me if I let you go."

"Don't worry about that. You leave him to me, José. Come on. What do you say?"

José didn't answer. He took his finger off the button, walked over to the couch, and sat down.

He studied a map of Spain he pinned on the wall. Below it was a framed picture of his family smiling at him. Margareta had her arms around him and their youngest of three sons.

He slid his phone out of his pocket and hit an icon. His brother, who was guarding the Kotmister estate in Spain, answered on the third ring. They talked.

"You cannot let him go. *Señor* Kotmister will find you and kill you," José's brother said.

"I think this *Señor* Reeves will kill him first. He is angry about his girlfriend."

"You have no guarantee he will pay you. He will turn you in, brother. We must stick to the plan. And tell your wife not to upset *Señor* Kotmister."

José sighed. *"Sí."*

Emma and Charles had adjoining suites at the Hilton in downtown Derby Crossing, Kentucky. While it was a beautiful place, she missed her condo, Millie, Maggie, and—Stratton.

She sat in the lotus position, her back against the couch, tapping on the iPad propped in front of her on the coffee table. In the past several months, Charles and Merek had insisted she learn to use more technology and they taught her well.

"We will find him, Miss H.," Merek's voice came through the speaker on Emma's iPhone, which sat on her shoulder, scrunched against her right ear.

"I know. Sorry about Calvin. He's a jerk, but I can't deal with work right now."

"No problem, Miss H."

"Hey, Merek?"

"Yes?"

"You know, I—"

"I know, you could not live without me. I know. I know. Hey, I gotta scram."

The call went dead. She shook her head as she set the iPhone on the table. Merek was the best business partner she could have, but his telephone manners ...

She surfed through the Mexican and Spanish restaurants within a fifty-mile radius of Derby Crossing. She found several on Facebook and posted a picture of Stratton to the pages with a reward for information.

She picked up her phone and hit the icon for Stratton's office in West Virginia at the *Stonefalls Post*.

"Stohhhhnefaaaahls Poooasht. How maaahy I heaalp yooooo?" Rhonda's West Virginia accent echoed in Emma's ear.

Rhonda was an elderly grandmother who came with the *Stonefalls Post* when Stratton bought it six years ago. She knew the newspaper business and ran it for Stratton since he moved into Emma's Clintonville condo. She and Stratton talked about moving into his house in Stonefalls, but they used it more as a getaway when Rhonda and her husband weren't there, doing the same.

"Hey, Rhonda, it's me."

"Oh, I'm so sorry, Miss Emma. I was reaching for something when I answered and didn't look to see the number. You won't tell …" She stopped.

No, I won't tell Stratton. She pictured Rhonda sitting at the front office oak desk wearing an orange polyester pantsuit, plastic orange jewelry, thirty pounds of makeup—including orange eye shadow and orange lipstick—all under a layer of perfume. Emma nearly coughed thinking of the smell.

"I'm sorry, Miss Emma, I just forget that, well, it's all so awful. Just awful. Have you found out anything good?"

"It's okay, Rhonda. Yes and no." She told Rhonda about the burnt truck. "How are things at the paper?"

"Slow. Slow. People stop in asking about Stratton. There's cards and calls coming in all the time. He's a popular man, you know. Loretta Caldwell even called askin' about him the other day. The nerve. The awful nerve of that woman after what happened between the two of you. She is a jealous evil woman, Miss Emma. Just awful jealous of you and Stratton. They should have put her in jail with her boyfriend when they had the chance."

Emma frowned. She didn't like the infamous man collector in Stonefalls who had a vengeful streak in her when it came to

Stratton any more than Rhonda. *Loretta Caldwell's name needs to go on that whiteboard.* "Well, she was found innocent, remember."

"Oh, well, at least that's what some people think. I think she was in on the whole heist when you and Stratton found out she had that necklace. It's just … Well, anyway. How are you holding up, honey?"

A wave of dread washed over her and she wiped a tear from her cheek. "I'm okay. I'm going to find him, Rhonda. I know I will."

"I know you will, too, honey. Oh, it's just awful."

"Yes, it is. Hey, I have to run. I'll talk to you soon. Just wanted to keep you up to date."

She ended the call before Rhonda could start talking again. She posted another reward for information and uploaded the picture of Stratton to another Facebook page. Her heart ached every time she looked at the picture that had appeared in all the media when he won his last award.

I wonder if I have a more recent picture, she thought and hit the *Photos* icon on her iPad. She tapped a small picture, and it grew on the screen. There sat Stratton smiling, sitting in his red kayak on the river in front of the boulder. It was the last picture she took of him. She zoomed in and moved it around to get his face in the center. It was too small, and he wore sunglasses. The picture she was using was better.

She was closing the picture when she noticed someone standing in the woods behind Stratton, as if they just stepped from behind a tree, looking straight at the camera. She enlarged the picture, and goose bumps rose on her arms.

Chapter 8

MARY SIPPED HER second martini, and Devereux nursed his first gin and tonic as they sat on her sunporch.

"I cannot believe Charles. This thing with Stratton should be handled by the authorities. Not by my only child," she snapped. She nearly slammed her glass on the table.

"But, darling, the man has been kidnapped and Charles is receiving the ransom calls. He can't just say, 'I'm sorry, I'm NOT taking your calls right now.' "

Mary glared at him. "I know that. It's just ... Oh, never mind," she slurred.

John pushed a cart into the room with their lunches, placed the salmon salads in front of them, and poured another martini from a pitcher into Mary's glass.

"Another drink so early in the day on an empty stomach?" Devereux asked.

Mary took a long sip and set the martini on the table. "Am I on trial in my own home?"

He reached for her hand. "I'm merely concerned about your well-being."

"Oh, are you now?"

"I love you. Of course, I want you to be healthy and happy."

"And rich?"

Devereux let go of her hand and lifted his drink, taking a small sip. He placed it back on the table and admired the beautiful landscaping and golf course beyond through the glass walls.

"Devereux, I have something serious to discuss with you."

"Of course, dear. What is it?" he smiled and patted her hand.

"I want to wear my pearl and ruby necklace at the wedding. You know, the necklace I wore the night we met," she slurred.

Silence. He took a large hit off his drink. "How divine. Yes, I do remember that necklace. You've not worn it since. It's beautiful. But perhaps we should discuss this another time."

"You mean when I'm not drunk." She laughed loudly, and her diamond engagement ring made a loud thud when she smacked the table. She continued. "I picked up my dress yesterday so I'll put the necklace on and make sure I don't have to buy another dress. It all must flow perfectly. Match. This wedding must be perfect. Perfect!" she yelled, giving him a sly look.

"Yes. It will be. But, well, you've ruined the surprise," he said, flustered.

Their eyes locked. He picked up his glass and finished it in two gulps.

She set her martini glass on the table and scowled at him through glassy eyes. He put his arm around the back of her chair, leaned into her, and whispered in her ear. "I am going to buy you the most beautiful strand of diamonds for our wedding day. Sparkling and voluptuous—like you."

She felt the butterflies in her stomach flapping—or was it the liquor? She nearly forgot how much she despised the liar and the thief. *What a shame. The only man I truly loved. So much for love.*

"I ruined it being a surprise for you. I'm so sorry," Mary said.

"It's all right." He finished his drink and waved the empty glass toward John, who was looking at them through the glass wall between the room and the kitchen.

John walked in and placed another drink in front of Devereux. "Everything to your liking?"

"Yes, thank you, John. As always, exquisite. The dressing is divine," Devereux said.

"That's John's secret recipe," Mary said as she lifted her glass toward John.

They ate for a while before Mary asked, "Can I have earrings to match?"

"That's a splendid idea."

"Yes, everything must match. Everything must be perfect for this wedding. Let's go over to see Dooney after we finish lunch."

"But dear, wouldn't it be better if we went another time? I don't think you're in any condition to pick out jewelry."

She eyed him while she chewed, swallowed, then asked, "Devereux, do you love me?"

"Of course, I love you."

"Is your divorce final yet?"

"Dear, this is just not a good time to —"

"No, it's not final. Who are we kidding? You don't want to marry me. You just want your French wife and your rich, famous, American golfer lover. That's it, isn't it?"

Devereux placed his knife and fork on the table, stood, and buttoned his jacket. "Mary, I believe it's best that we discuss this matter later. If you'll excuse me, I need to make a call."

Mary looked up and pointed at him with her fork. "No, Devereux. You will sit down this second and don't you ever speak to me like that again. Ever. Do you understand? And after we finish our lunch you are taking me to Dooney's and buying me my necklace and matching pair of diamond earrings. Do you understand, darling?"

Mary glanced at the tabloid and tossed it on the glass table-top. She expected to be on the cover again soon, especially after she and Deverux had their final knockout yelling match at the airport as he left her limo. Devereux feigned a business emergency based on a call he received during their shopping at Dooney's. She didn't remember him taking a call, but then again, in her state after three martinis, she doubted she remembered everything during the afternoon. She was relieved that he had enough sense to leave. Otherwise, she would've told him to leave. But she wasn't through with him yet. *No, not in the least.*

Her driver had politely tried to put her back in the car, but she refused, yelling at Devereux's back as he walked through the terminal doors with paparazzi likely lurking nearby. She did enjoy seeing herself in the media and felt the edges of her mouth turn up. At least she had been the one yelling. *No one messes with Mary Wellington II.*

She came home and took a long nap—or perhaps she actually just passed out. She sipped a glass of lemon water, looking out the windows at her golf course. She wasn't leaving here and certainly not with Devereux. She divorced Charles's father and rebuilt this estate the way she wanted—on her terms—no one else's.

It struck her how entranced she was with Devereux, but she still didn't understand why she fell in love with him. But it was time to take a stand and remove Devereux from her life once and for all.

She knew that she would make a spectacle of him, but she still hadn't figured out the details. She pictured many scenarios since he slipped the necklace into his pocket. One of them made her giddy with excitement. Within days, she went from wedding plans to *devastate-Devereux-plans*. She strode to the wall and pushed an intercom button.

"John, would you please draw me a bath and make sure the jets are on high. I need to soak for a bit."

"Certainly."

She walked back to the table, sat down, and picked up her iPhone. She hit the speed dial icon for Charles's new number. She thought it to go straight to voice mail again when he answered on the second ring.

"Yes, Mother?"

"Charles, I need to speak with you."

"What is it? I cannot leave Kentucky right now so—"

"I know that." She paused. "Devereux and I had a huge argument."

"Really?"

"Don't sound so pleased."

"Mother, it doesn't matter to me who you keep company with."

"It most certainly does and you know it."

Silence. "Do you need to talk about it?"

"No. I won't bore you with the details. Could Merek look into something for me?"

A long pause from Charles before he replied. "Mother, we're rather busy dealing with a kidnapping, in case that slipped your mind." He paused. "Something as in what?"

"Nothing that concerns you. Just a background check on a security guard who's applied for employment."

"That's odd. Why not have Kevin do it for you?"

"He can't know about it. You understand."

"Mother, are you firing him?"

"I cannot tolerate inefficiency. You know that."

"But Kevin's been the head of your security for years. You'll be hard-pressed to find a replacement."

"My point exactly. That's why I want this applicant checked out to the fullest."

"What's the applicant's name, and I'll pass the information on to Merek."

"I'll call him myself. Just give me his number."

"I'll text it to you. It's in my other phone. I don't have it committed to memory."

"Fine. That would be lovely. How are you?"

"I'm extremely busy and terribly stressed. I haven't had a decent night's sleep since Emma called me last Saturday. This entire ordeal is beyond belief."

"Yes, I can imagine. And Stratton Reeves is such a handsome man. What a shame."

Emma had taken Stratton to Mary's Christmas gala. She told Charles that she got a kick out of watching Mary turn on her charms around Stratton. But Stratton had only pulled Emma closer to him. Mary looked miffed and floated away to light upon another man, like a bee seeking flowers.

Charles, as always, was embarrassed about Mary's normal behavior. But she wasn't going to change.

"What a shame he's been kidnapped or what a shame Emma got to him before you did?"

"Oh, darling. Don't talk such nonsense." She took another sip of her water, which helped ease her headache. "Although it does amaze me what he sees in her. They have nothing in common. She's too young for him. Emma and that kayaking. And see where that got him. The poor man."

"Is there anything else you want to discuss? I really should go."

"I understand, dear. Devereux had to go back to France. I'm going to be dreadfully lonely. Please come home soon and spend time with me."

"We'll talk later."

"Kisses and hugs to you, darling. Toodles."

"Goodbye."

Seconds later, her phone buzzed with Charles's text. She tapped on Merek's number.

"Hello," Merek answered.

"Mr. Polanski, this is Mary Wellington, Charles's mother." They made small talk for several seconds before she got to the point.

"I would like you to do an extensive background check on someone for me."

He paused. "Sure thing, Mrs. Wellington."

Mary admired his Polish accent, reminding her of a golfer from Poland she dated in her forties whom she hadn't thought of in decades. She blushed. She made a mental note to look him up.

"I need information on my fiancé, Devereux."

"The picture maker from France?"

"Yes. I need everything and anything you can find out about him, and I need it quickly. And keep this strictly between you and me. Don't mention it to anyone. Not Charles. Not Emma. No one."

"Sure thing, Mrs. Wellington. Hey, I gotta scram."

The call went dead in Mary's ear.

"How horribly rude," she said to the phone with a frown.

"José. Answer me!" Stratton yelled toward the mirrors one last time before he resumed pacing the living room. He had to remain calm, keep up his strength, and look for any opportunity that presented itself to escape. But he was growing restless, and he couldn't count on José to help him.

He sat down and began reading the latest issue of the *Derby Crossing Herald* again. The media seemed to have forgotten about the case, or it could be the authorities had clamped down on the media. Doubtful. The public was inundated with tragedy after tragedy. Stratton's kidnapping had gone cold, which meant they may have given him up for dead. Dead like his Emma. Again he thought it odd nothing had ever been mentioned about her accident. No story. No obituary.

But based on the accident, it may have been decided to forgo the ordinary. The entire ordeal was far from ordinary. He imagined Charles and Merek discussing the situation and likely helping with the investigation. Or was she still alive in a hospital unconscious, while they were sat at her bedside?

He knew he could overtake Dayton, but José would shoot him before he could make the move. He wasn't as quick as he used to be and knew his limits. And there could be more people behind the glass with José. He couldn't tell. He had to stay alive to escape.

Stratton knew he struck a nerve with Dayton's ego about the autobiography. He would play on that as much as he could. It could keep him alive.

He'd have Kotmister take him to places of his youth or where he burned down the estate. *Where he met my dear, young Emma.* He squeezed back tears. He had to get outside this prison. He needed to talk to the police, Charles, Merek, and Rhonda. One of them more than likely had Maggie. His heart lifted slightly at the thought of his beautiful, rescued golden retriever running through his mountainside yard in West Virginia. The home he and his deceased wife had built together.

Stratton's thoughts were interrupted by Dayton waltzing through the metal door, like many times for the past five days.

"You'll be saying goodbye to America very soon. I'll have a bag packed for you. You just be dressed and ready to leave the premises."

Stratton tossed the newspaper on a side table and got to his feet. "What?"

"We'll be going to my resort soon. You'll have everything you need there. In fact, you may just like it so much … Let's not get ahead of ourselves. I've not nailed down the exact time."

Stratton sat down in one of the chairs. Dayton's toothpick body folded down across from him.

"And what if I refuse to go?"

"Come now. Let's not be silly. It's tiresome. We're both too intelligent for such games. Explain to me how this book process will work. I assume we'll talk about when I was born or start with my great-grandfather. He did start the company. I did hate burning down that house, but I needed the cash. I admit it was a stupid thing to do. Well, we won't put *everything* in the book. I suppose you've always wanted to write a book about the criminal mind?"

"No. Actually, about the building of a giant family financial firm like Kotmister's."

"Really?" Dayton sat back in the chair. "Then it appears you're in luck. They say everything happens for a reason, now don't they? But I always felt that everything happened for money."

Stratton scowled at him.

"Anyway, how long will it take to finish my book?"

"It shouldn't take long, with my connections. Once it's written maybe six months, tops."

Kotmister raised his head and his eyebrows at the same time. He reminded Stratton of the jack-o'-lantern he and Emma had made together. What a fun evening it had been, drinking Emma's favorite wine, Côtes du Rhône, and carving the pumpkin. It was right after they returned from Chillicothe. The pain rushed over him like a wave and he suddenly felt nauseous—again. He stood and walked to the far side of the room to shake it off.

"You know, Mr. Reeves. Your taste in women is questionable, but your knowledge of writing is splendid. I like this idea. Certainly. Oh, yes, this will be fantastic. Don't you think so, José?" Dayton spoke upward toward the one-way mirrors.

"*Sí, Señor Kotmister. Fantastico,*" came the voice through the speakers.

Dayton grinned. "So, how do we begin?"

"I've been thinking about this, and it would be best if we visited places of your youth and places where important events happened in your life. Interviewing you at those places will trigger more memories and improve the quality of your legacy." *I won't let Dayton get me on that plane.*

Dayton's eyes flicked back and forth as if he were looking for traffic at a busy crosswalk. He tapped his right index finger against his chin as he closed his eyes for several moments. He opened them and asked, "Improve my legacy, you say?"

"Yes. Very much so. That's the best process. Visit the places. If I'm going to write this book it's got to be the best it can be. I, too, have a reputation to keep."

Kotmister stood and ran his fingers through his gelled hair as he walked around like a long-legged heron stepping carefully from rock to rock. "I do miss my home. But let me think it over. In the meantime we can get started on my interview now."

"I'll need a computer."

"Can't you jot this down on paper or something? Wait. I don't believe there's a scrap of paper or a pen here. I'll have a laptop and all those sorts of writing things you may need delivered in the morning. Just talk to José if there's anything else you need."

"I'll do that," Stratton said, glancing up at the mirrors.

Chapter 9

"Can you zoom in on it more, please?" Emma asked, standing in front of the huge digital screen at the Derby Crossing police station.

"Sure," a young officer said, sitting at the conference table, moving the computer's mouse and clicking a few times. "We enlarged the pixels, refocused, and cropped it to just this area."

A thin man with blond hair faced the camera. He was dressed in a camo shirt and pants, holding a pair of binoculars about chest height, as if he just lowered them.

She tilted her head and took several steps back, examined it, then looked down at the floor. She shook her head, looked up, frowned, and studied the screen. "It can't be him. He's in prison."

"Who? It can't be who, Ms. Haines? Do you know the man in the picture?" Arnold asked.

"It looks like Dayton Kotmister."

"Kotmister?" Charles asked, jumping to his feet and joining her. "The arsonist who took a shot at you when you were at Matrix and flipped his Ferrari trying to flee the scene?"

"Yes."

Charles and Emma told the agents the story. While Emma was doing a claims exam of the burnt Kotmister estate in August of 2006, Dayton Kotmister had shown up out of nowhere. When Emma asked him questions and, basically, told him she knew he was lying, Kotmister took off with Emma in hot pursuit.

She managed to call Joey right before Dayton bolted and when Joey's black-and-white charged up the drive, Kotmister flipped his red Ferrari trying to go around them. He was booked and sent to prison.

"This the rich Kotmister kid of Kotmister Financial? The one all obsessed with horses and gambling?" Jay asked. "The one you helped bust with Detective Reed?"

"The one and the same," Emma said.

"You chased him?" Arnold asked, grinning at Emma.

"I didn't think about him having a gun. I just ran after him. That part isn't in the report that I'm sure you've already read."

"What happened?"

She rolled her eyes and blushed. "I tripped over a rock, and the bullet went over my head into the company car. I was lucky. That's when I quit Matrix and field work and started my own business. I thought it would be safer. So much for that."

"We'll start a full rundown on Kotmister. Good work, Ms. Haines. Hold on a minute." Jay made a call on his cellphone.

"You chased him?" Arnold asked Emma again, smiling and walking closer to her. She shrugged.

"Ms. Haines, you could be right. Kotmister was released in 2009," Jay said, walking up beside her.

Emma turned to Charles, who had slumped down in his chair. "Kotmister was Simon's investor, right? I saw him before I busted him with you and Simon at a party years ago. I saw Simon introduce you to him when I was coming back from the ladies' room. But I never met him. He glanced at me, but I never really met him. And Simon left … for Spain."

Charles nodded, his chin resting in his hand. "Yes. That's correct." He lowered his hand as his left pinkie finger twitched.

"And didn't he ask you out a few times?" Emma continued.

"More than a few. He became an utter nuisance." Charles said softly.

"Simon Johnson, your former partner, moved to … Spain?" Arnold asked.

"Yes," Charles said.

"I bet that Simon gave Kotmister Charles's cell number. And Simon knew when Charles and I kayaked the Red every year and told him that, too. It all makes sense now," she said, shaking her head. She gave Charles a sad look. *So he left Charles for Kotmister.*

"He meant to kidnap Charles, but he had to take Stratton instead. I just happened to be walking toward him while he was in that truck and he ran over me."

"Sounds reasonable," Arnold agreed, nodding.

"Hard to believe Simon would be involved with Kotmister, but people change. We all know that. But the three of us were friends and …" She motioned to Charles who looked flattened.

"Simon would never be involved in such a thing," Charles said weakly.

"How do you know?" Jay asked.

"I just know."

"Kotmister's out and he's got it in for you and Stratton and Miss Haines. And we need to find Simon Johnson," Jay said.

"He doesn't have it in for me. I'm already dead," Emma said.

Emma sat on the couch in the hotel suite and sipped a bottle of Smeraldina water she found in the fridge.

"Do you have reason to believe that our father is still alive?" Glen Reeves asked into her ear.

"Because when we talked with the FBI investigators yesterday, they sounded skeptical," his sister, Ellen, added. The three of them were on a conference call.

"He's still alive," Emma said.

"But how do you know? This Kotmister character sounds like a crazy and dangerous man," Glen said.

"I just do." Emma said, stretching out on the couch and closing her eyes. *Do I really?*

"Emma, I can understand how you feel, but I'm not sure you're being realistic. You know as well as I do that a kidnap victim's chances of survival drop by the second. It's been days since Father was taken and they can't find him," Glen said.

"I'm sure we'll find him. Alive."

"We're both flying in tonight for the review meeting with the FBI in the morning. I'm too upset to do much right now anyway, so I may as well stay there for a while. Ramesh will just have to take over some of my more critical surgeries," Ellen said.

Stratton's daughter, Ellen, was Emma's age and had two grown children. Laura was in law school at Harvard and Jason was studying journalism at Yale. Stratton was proud of his family and happy that someone had decided to follow in his journalism footsteps. She and her husband, a handsome doctor from India, Dr. Ramesh Gupta, had a surgery practice in Manhattan.

Glen was a year younger and also a surgeon in New York, specializing in hand surgery. He married a power attorney, Clarisse, who was a partner at one of the law firms in New York. They also had a girl and a boy. Haley was a fourteen-year-old beauty and violin virtuoso. Todd was a sixteen-year-old lacrosse champion and track star at his high school.

Stratton spent many weekends in New York attending his grandchildren's events and visiting. He often stayed at Glen's with his grandchildren while Glen and Clarisse jetted off to a faraway country for a long weekend.

Emma had met the entire family around Christmas. It seemed to her that all his kids did was cut people up and sew them back together, twenty-four hours, seven days a week. She once tried to imagine their conversations around the dinner table, but thought better of it.

While Stratton told her his family was happy about their relationship she had an idea of what they really thought. Right now she felt like she was in the hot seat—again. Stratton's disappearance happening so soon after his being shot and wounded when he was helping her solve the case in Chillicothe last October couldn't be in her favor. And then there were the circumstances when she met Stratton in West Virginia.

She knew they had concerns about their father shacking up with a woman who was their age and sometimes found trouble when her kayak hit the water.

"I'll see you tomorrow then," Emma said.

"Fine," Glen said and left the call.

"I hope you're getting enough rest and taking care of yourself. I know this has been a horrible experience for you," Ellen said.

"You, too. It's been hard on all of us. But at least we know who it is now and we're going to bring your dad home safe. We will."

"I'll pay you anything you want, José. And you'll be out from under Dayton Kotmister for good. I can do it. I'm a rich man. All I want is for you to just help me get out of here. It's that simple. No cops. No nothing. I'll take care of Dayton. Your name won't ever be mentioned. You and your wife can get on with your lives and live in total freedom. I can get the money for you to do that. Come down here, and we'll discuss it. Man to man," Stratton said toward the one-way mirrors before he wiped his lips with a napkin. He was tired of talking with José like this, but he felt it was necessary and he was guessing José might carry a cellphone.

He was also frustrated that he didn't know Joey's, Merek's, Charles's, Emma's, or even his own cell numbers. They were all in his phone he left in Emma's truck. Technology had its drawbacks. But 911 would be his number of choice as soon as he got a phone.

He ate his scrambled eggs and took a drink of orange juice. He checked the new laptop sitting on the desk that had been delivered during the night and, of course, no Wi-Fi access.

He thought of the many dangerous situations working decades as a journalist both stateside and abroad after returning from Vietnam. *And I end up being held hostage, not far from my own home, snatched on a kayak trip in Kentucky.*

"One never knows what will flip you out of your boat on the river of life," Emma had said to him. The feeling of his heart sinking again was suddenly interrupted by a voice through the speakers above his head.

"Any sum of money, *Señor*?" José asked.

Stratton stood, shoved the chair up to the table, and looked up at the mirrors. "Look, we've been through this several times, José. Just—"

The metal door to the room opened and Kotmister strolled in, coffee cup in hand.

"Good morning, Mr. Reeves. I see you've made yourself a little something to eat. Good. Good. Keep up your strength. You need to have a clear head while we're working on my memoir. Shall we resume where we left off?"

Stratton threw his napkin on the table and walked over to what had become his chair. Dayton dropped into the chair across from him—into *his* chair. The thought of spending time with Dayton Kotmister made Stratton want to place his already eaten breakfast in Kotmister's lap. He held the thought for several seconds.

Kotmister would be appalled at the mess, and Stratton could take him. But he still wasn't sure whose side José was on or if he could force himself to throw up. He put the thought in the back of his mind.

"Where should we begin?" Kotmister asked, smiling.

"Did you bring the recorder?"

"Ah, yes. Here." Kotmister jumped out of the chair and handed a small hand-held recorder to Stratton. He tested it and placed it on the table between them. Kotmister returned to his seat.

"I'm going to record all of this, as we discussed."

Dayton gestured for him to begin. Stratton pressed the record button, "Maybe we should start from the present time and go backward. While it's still fresh in everyone's mind. Then we'll go to your young adulthood, back to teenager, to childhood. How's that sound?"

"I thought we were starting with my childhood. Where I was born? What a privileged life I led as a Kotmister? Go from there? Weave in the family history?"

Stratton shook his head. "No. I've been thinking this over. By going back, I think it will trigger more memories about your childhood. Those memories are usually buried pretty deep. Did you buy your notebook as I instructed?"

"Yes. Yes, I did. It's right here in my pocket." Dayton patted his pocket, excitedly, like a little boy with a new toy in his pocket.

"And have you made any notes in it yet?"

"Just one."

"And?"

"Ahhh, yes." He pulled the notebook out of his pocket and flipped it open.

"It says that we are to be at the county airport at five in the morning."

Stratton frowned, squinted, and shook his head. "What?"

"That's when the plane will be there to take us to Spain," Dayton said. "Oh, don't look so glum, Mr. Reeves. You'll love staying at my villa. I'll even bring you some lovely women. You'll soon forget about that dead girlfriend of yours. You may like it so much you'll decide to work for me."

Stratton stared at him.

"Now, where should we start?"

"Let's start with your scheme for all of this—the full story." Stratton gestured around the room.

"You mean like a confession, of sorts."

"Of sorts," Stratton said.

Kotmister sat back in his chair, a broad smile on his face. "I actually like the idea. Yes, I would like to talk about it. But it's not going in the book, of course. Turn the recorder off." He pointed to it on the table. Stratton picked it up and turned it off. He showed it to Dayton. Dayton nodded. As Stratton set the recorder back on the table, he flipped it back on, making sure the little green light was hidden from Dayton.

Dayton told his story while Stratton suppressed the desire to jump up and choke his broomstick neck.

"Simon Johnson came to me about managing his investments years ago. Simon was handsome and rich. My type. I have to say, Mr. Reeves, have you ever seen someone and the first time you saw them, you knew you wanted to be with them? They call it love at first sight."

Stratton glared at him. He felt that way when Emma walked into his office nine months ago. He grew up with Ann, and they married young. She died of cancer six years ago. And now Emma. *Both gone.* He shifted in his chair.

Dayton rolled his eyes. "Never mind. This isn't about you. It's about me." Stratton felt the urge to kick him in the face and watch it shatter, but sat as still as a hiding cat. It was the only way he could control his anger.

"Let's see. Oh, yes. When I saw Simon, I wanted him. And I was going to have him. I tried everything to split them up. Even chased Charles a bit, but he's such an intellectual snob. I have no idea what Simon saw in him. Anyway—"

"Simon Johnson? Charles's partner?"

"Yes. To your point—he was with Charles. But I pursued Simon for some time. He was quite firm with me about his loyalty to his relationship and, I have to say, that made me want him even more. But there was no convincing him. He finally told me that if I ever contacted him again he would have a restraining order put against me." Dayton burst into loud laughter.

Stratton flinched.

"I mean, me. Really?" He gestured to himself with his long fingers and laughed harder. "Please. Dayton Kotmister. One of the richest men in the world. You not only deny me? You threaten me? Needless to say, this did not sit well with me at all."

"I can imagine."

"Oh, Mr. Reeves. You have no idea. I decided to destroy them. If you can't have them, destroy them, is my motto."

"Sounds like a bumper sticker."

"That's an excellent idea. I'll have some printed. Let me go on."

"Please do."

"I told Simon that if he didn't leave Charles and come and live with me in Spain and never contact Charles again, I would kill Charles."

The room was silent for several seconds.

"So you ruined both their lives," Stratton said.

"Of course, silly. Don't you see? If I can't get what I want and it serves me no purpose, I destroy it. Simon snuck off last October and tried to see Charles again. But he was stopped in the nick of time." Dayton chuckled.

"And where is Simon now?"

Dayton sniffed and looked at the ceiling. "We'll get to that."

"So you've held Simon as a prisoner for almost four years?"

"I wouldn't call him a prisoner, really. I gave him a choice and he made it."

"Is he there because he wants to be there or he's being forced? There seems to be a trend here."

Kotmister shrugged.

"Why doesn't he try to escape or kill you?"

Dayton chuckled. "Oh, Mr. Reeves. I said we'll get to him later."

Stratton glared at him.

"Let's talk about my childhood. It was wonderful. Did you know I used to have pony parties? Only I had Saddlebred parties. Beautiful horses, American Saddlebreds. You know, it will be fun to remember my life."

"Let's continue talking about Simon," Stratton said sternly.

"Mr. Reeves, may I remind you that you're in no position to tell me what to do." He snapped his fingers and the red dot appeared on Stratton's shirt.

Stratton looked down, then up, and said quite loudly, "So you let other people do all your dirty work and you'll let them go to prison for you."

"I pay them enough that they make sure no one goes to prison, especially me—not again."

"You pay them to spend the rest of their lives under your thumb. They're already prisoners."

"They wouldn't make that kind of money doing honest work. They're not bright enough. I make them very wealthy."

The room went still. Stratton hoped José was absorbing every word.

Stratton's lip curled over his teeth. "You are one sick son of—"

"Now, now, Mr. Reeves. Let's not use foul language." He waved his long finger back and forth in front of Stratton's face and made a "tsk-tsk" sound. He looked at his watch. "I have a meeting. We'll continue this conversation on the plane in the morning."

And with that, Kotmister stood, turned, punched in the key code, and walked out the metal door. Stratton leaned over the table, switched off the recorder, and slid it into his pocket.

Chapter 10

DEVEREUX KISSED AMELIA'S young neck as he fastened Mary's necklace around it. The ruby sparkled at the base of her throat.

She admired her reflection in the mirror, sliding her hands across her newly acquired jewels. "You spoil me." She giggled.

"You're worth it."

"And you flew right back, just because you missed me?"

"Absolutely, my love." He turned her around, raised her chin, and kissed her before he drew away. He went into the walk-in closet, shrugged into a shirt, and stood behind Amelia, buttoning it.

"I have a few things to work on in my office. Please don't disturb me," he said to her reflection in the mirror.

"That's fine," she said, dreamily. "I'll go shopping then."

"Yes. You do that. You buy such lovely things that look smashing on you, my dear."

He left her petting her new necklace as if she were in a trance. She was beautiful, childlike, and downright dumb. Still, the younger ones pleased him more in bed.

He went into his office and locked the door. He fired up his iMac and scrolled through his latest emails. He read them intently before he closed the site and opened the folder with the long password. He double clicked on the first Word document, increased the numbers, and printed out the financial statement. He did this for the next thirty clients. They were always pleased with the fifty-percent returns. *The ignorant jerks. Being rich and famous obviously doesn't mean you're smart.*

His iPhone buzzed, and he picked it up.

"Yes, I'm sending them out today."

"I thought you were in America with the golfer."

Devereux frowned. "I was until yesterday afternoon. We had a misunderstanding, but nothing I can't repair. I need to get a few more things into place in Boston before I tie the knot with Mary."

"You know best about how to build the relationships with our investors. I'm merely the bookkeeper. Speaking of which, we received twenty million from our clients in Hollywood last evening."

"Perfect."

There was a tap on the door.

"I have to go. Everything is fine. We'll meet for dinner tonight. Be here at, say, seven," he spoke rapidly in French.

"Fine. We'll see you then."

Devereux ended the call and set the iPhone on his desk. "Yes, dear?" he said toward the door. "Just a minute."

He slid the stack of financial statements into the top drawer of the desk, walked to the door, and opened it.

"Honey, I can't find my keys. Can I take your car?"

"Certainly."

He pulled the keys to the Mercedes from his pocket and handed them to her, kissing her cheek. "Just be home for dinner tonight. Regal and Leslie will be here at seven."

She smiled and nodded, glancing toward his computer screen. "What are you working on?"

"Just boring movie legalities."

"When can I see one of your movies?"

"Soon, darling. I'm going to have a showing in a few months. This documentary on the history of golfing is difficult. Golfers have quite demanding schedules. It's hard to get time with them and my camera crew together. The place, the lighting, everything must be perfect."

"Can we have the golfers over for dinner sometime?"

"When the documentary's completed we'll throw a big party. How's that?"

"Oh, Devie. I love parties."

"Yes, dear. I know. Now, run along." He cupped a hand to his ear. "I think I hear Kate Spade calling."

She giggled and waved as he closed the door behind her, locked it, leaned against it, and rolled his eyes.

At least the older ones have a brain.

Mary put a ball on the tee and whacked it. It bounced near the next hole. She handed her caddy the club and he placed it in the bag. As they started to walk her cell vibrated in her pocket and she answered.

"Darling. Hello."

"Hello, Mother."

"It's a shame you're not here. It's such a lovely day. While the world around is crumbling, you could be here on the course caddying for me."

"I try to focus on the positive in the world."

"And what is that? Kayaking and work and moving away to Switzerland? I do think that's the best thing for you—your moving. I've been thinking about it a great deal. We'll just have to fly more to see one another. After all, you're here and I never see you anymore anyway."

Charles didn't answer.

"Charles, this will not wait any longer. I need to discuss Devereux with you. We're planning to marry, and I'm selling the estate and moving to France."

"You can't be serious."

She tilted her head back. "Actually, you're right. I'm not. Not anymore."

"Excuse me? What are you talking about?"

"I need you to help me. I received a call earlier this morning from your friend, Merek. What a rude young man, but it seems he can find out anything about anyone."

"He found out about the security guard?"

"What security guard?"

"The one you requested information about."

"Security guard?"

"You're not making any sense. The guard you wanted Merek to investigate to replace Kevin."

"Oh, yes. Never mind that. There was no security guard. It was all about my beloved," she said, her red lipstick curling up at the edges. "I have a little plan for my wedding, but I will need the help of your police friend, Joey."

"Mother, what on earth are you talking about?"

She explained her plan, ended the call, and made another call to Detective Joey Reed, as Charles and Merek had suggested.

"Devereux, darling. I'm so sorry I blew up at the airport like I did. Forgive me?" Mary said, rolling her eyes, a hand on her hip. "I want to get married now—as soon as possible. I don't want to wait. Your leaving made me realize this more than ever, my love." She yawned and examined her red manicured fingernails.

"Mary, my dear. I've missed you, too. Of course, I forgive you. I'm sorry. You want to get married soon, you say?" Devereux's voice came through the small speakerphone. The sound echoed through Mary's sunroom.

"Yes. And forget the prenuptial papers. I mean it." Mary waved her arm theatrically as if she were onstage. "Did she sign the divorce papers?"

A long pause. "Not yet. She's making this quite difficult, my dear." Another pause. "I have to go to Boston for a few months for a documentary I'm shooting there. Unfortunately, I've already made commitments and many people are involved. The earliest I can be back is August. I'm sure that she'll sign the papers by then and my documentary will be at a point I can return to you, my dear."

"I see. Well, let's get married here in August then. Right here. Before Charles leaves for Switzerland. A huge party. I'll have John help me with everything. We'll have the biggest, most lovely wedding ever. It will be in all the papers and magazines. I'll invite every photographer from all over the world. It will be our day." Mary tilted her head back and closed her eyes toward the ceiling.

Another long pause. "Actually, I believe we should have a small private affair."

"No. I won't hear of it. I love you, and I cannot wait to be your wife and tell the world. Everyone in the world will know we're married."

Another long pause. "Very well, then. August it is. We'll set a date. I'll be there as quickly as I can. You understand."

"Yes, of course. I'm on tour the next several weeks myself in California. But after that, do hurry back, Devereux, darling. Toodles." She lowered the phone, hit the end call icon, tossed it on the table, and sat down in a dining room chair. She exhaled a large sigh.

"So you want me to arrest him during the ceremony?" Joey asked again with a look on his face as if he just swallowed the dill pickle that sat on his plate.

She picked up her napkin, removed the silverware, placed it on the table, and draped the napkin over her lap. She speared a piece of melon from the crystal dessert bowl with her fork, raised it, and twirled it as if she were inspecting a jewel. "Absolutely. And make it a grand event. My security people will be in plain clothes inside and outside the estate. He can't escape if he tries."

Joey took another bite of his turkey, Swiss, and avocado sandwich with freshly made raspberry jam on thick slices of bread that John had pulled from the oven. He wondered if he ever had a sandwich that tasted as good. It was nothing like the ones he fixed or bought. Maybe he could ask John to make him a few and freeze them, but that thought was replaced by the situation at hand. He finished chewing, wiped his mouth, and picked up his iced tea.

"We've contacted five of the seven women he's married. They've all agreed to press charges. This man must be quite the ladies' man. Seven wives, going on number eight." He shook his head. "Makes me tired to think about it. I'll have him tailed when he gets off the plane in Boston."

Mary said nothing. She looked down at her plate and cut into her sandwich with her knife and fork as if she had to kill it.

They ate in silence. John came into the room carrying a pitcher of what appeared to be tomato juice with crushed ice. He poured it in a tall glass and added a celery stick and a dash of nutmeg.

"I used the Grey Goose as you instructed."

"John, you're a good man," Mary said, reaching across the table and patting his arm.

John placed the pitcher on the table and turned to Joey.

"Would you like a Bloody Mary as well, sir?"

Joey shook his head. "No, thanks. Not while I'm on the clock. But I have to tell you, this is the finest sandwich I've ever eaten in my life and I've eaten my share."

"Thank you, Detective Reed. It's a recipe my wife and I have mastered over the years. We bake the bread fresh and grill it in a special marinade of butter and spices. We think that's the secret."

"Whatever it is, I wouldn't mind having a few dozen of these in my freezer."

John frowned and jerked back. "Absolutely not! If you froze them they would be ruined. I take pride in making everything fresh, grown by local farmers, and serving it as quickly as possible."

Joey blinked and glanced at Mary.

"Now, if you'll excuse me. I'm preparing duck for dinner." John left the room.

"Great guy. Gets a little testy about his food, though. How'd you find him?"

"I put an ad in the local paper. John and his wife have been with me for over fifty years. And to think I was going to let them go for Devereux." She picked up the Bloody Mary and took a healthy swig before placing it gently back onto the table. "I cannot wait to see the look on his face when he's arrested. And I'll invite all the Mrs. Devereuxs from all over the world to watch." Her eyes glimmered.

"I'll tell you one thing, Ms. Wellington. This will be a first, and I've been a cop for a long time." He took another drink of his iced tea—also perfect. Freshly brewed. Not too tart. Not too sweet.

"It will be a first for everyone, Detective Reed."

Emma, Charles, Agent Jay, two local police officers, Ellen, and Glen were in the Derby Crossing police station conference room watching Agent Arnold pace in front of them, pointing at the whiteboard behind him for the past hour.

"And that's where we stand today. Questions?"

"I don't understand why you can't just find him. I'm sorry. I cannot comprehend this. You *are* the FBI," Glen said.

His voice sounded so much like Stratton's it made Emma's heart ache. Glen moved like his father, too.

"We will catch him. It's just a matter of time. He'll slip up again. We have the entire area covered with our best people. His calls have already been located to come from around here. That's a slip-up. His getting in Ms. Haines's picture on the river was a major slip-up."

Ellen raised a slender hand. "Do you think our father is still alive? Truthfully."

The room went still.

Charles glanced at Emma. She turned away. "There's no evidence to prove that he is or isn't alive. We can't answer that question. I'm sorry," Arnold said softly.

"And your former partner, Simon Johnson, is in on this?" Glen turned in his chair to Charles.

Charles glared at him. "There is no reason to determine that Simon is even in close proximity to Dayton Kotmister or has been in contact with him for years."

"But he was your investment advisor. Wouldn't that give *you* a reason to know about him?"

"I didn't know him at all. He did no investing for me. He was Simon's personal investor. We kept our investments separate."

"But you said before that you knew the kidnapper." Glen pounded him.

"I met him very briefly at a party he was hosting. Emma accompanied us to the party. But she wasn't there when the introductions were being made. She excused herself before Kotmister came over to Simon and me."

Glen looked at Emma, then raised an eyebrow at Agent Arnold. He turned back to Charles.

"And then he kept chasing after you, from what we've been told here."

"Yes. But I never saw him other than that single occasion at that party with Simon. He called and emailed me, asking to meet him for dinner. But I always declined."

Glen turned to Emma. "You certainly run with an interesting crowd."

"I don't *run* with anyone, Glen. I met Dayton Kotmister when I busted him. I didn't even meet him at the party. I hardly call that running around with him."

Tension surged through the room. Arnold quickly interrupted. "We've contacted Kotmister's former business colleagues. Appears he has no living family. He's been living at a hidden location in Spain, and we've contacted the authorities there. They have their best people on it."

"Do you think my father could be in Spain?" Ellen asked.

Agent Jay explained that every airport record from the surrounding area for the past several weeks had been scrubbed, but they all came up empty. Gaining information from private jet companies required a subpoena which the FBI had already obtained, but they came up cold there, too. "Criminals can find ways around anything—especially rich ones," Jay concluded.

"As you've been told, we cannot determine the exact location of Mr. Reeves, but we do believe that Dayton Kotmister is at a location in this area based on his text and phone call to Mr. Wellington. We're going with the assumption that Mr. Reeves is with him," Arnold said.

"And you heard a horse in the background on the last call," Ellen added.

"Yes. That is correct," Agent Jay said.

"But that was days ago. He could be long gone by now. And your former partner didn't mention anything to you about his investor? Where he lived? What he did? Nothing?" Glen asked Charles again, his voice rising.

"As I've told you and the authorities, I know nothing about Dayton Kotmister other than the facts I've already shared. I'm not on trial here, Mr. Reeves," Charles said, coldly.

Emma laid her head atop her crossed arms on the desk in front of her. Everyone thought Stratton was dead. Even she was beginning to lose faith. Hearing Stratton's own flesh and blood ask the questions made her chest well up into her throat. She felt dizzy and needed to get out of the room. She got up and walked into the hallway. Charles slipped out of his seat and followed her.

She moved a chair to face a long window and sat with her legs curled under her. Cars buzzed up and down the freeway. *Is he still out there somewhere?*

Charles leaned on the wall and looked out the window, too. A few seconds passed before he walked behind her and squeezed her shoulders, leaving his hands there to rest.

Emma sat at the kitchen table in the suite at the Derby Crossing Hilton, swiping her iPad.

"What on earth are you doing?" Charles asked, sipping a bottle of Perrier as he sat in a chair beside the couch. His cell was on the table in front of him.

"Posting Dayton Kotmister's ugly mug on every Facebook page I can find around here. Since he's such a horse freak, I even emailed all the farms around here that I could find, too."

"Don't you think the FBI has already done that? And if Kotmister thinks you're dead, don't you want to keep the fact that you're alive hidden?"

"Merek thought of that. He put a memorial on my Facebook page and set up an anonymous account and email for me, too. And if the FBI did do postings, I really don't care. I'm doing them, too. I'm not sure many people would call the FBI and want to get involved. And Merek is recalling all the auto accessory stores."

"I see. Merek is quite clever, especially when it comes to computer issues."

She stopped tapping on her screen and set the iPad on the table.

"Yeah. He is one sharp Polish cookie. I don't think I could survive without him. I don't think H.I.T. would survive. He's pretty amazing. I lucked out when I met him." She balled her hands in her hair, pulled it, then sighed and looked at Charles. "Don't you remember anything about Dayton? Like where he hung out or who he hung out with? Who was at that party? Who he might know down here?"

Charles shook his head. "I wish I did. But I only met him once, and I knew I never wanted to see him again. I have no idea why Simon would give him a cent, but I didn't advise Simon about how to invest his money."

"Hey, I'm sorry that Glen grilled you."

Charles shrugged and took another drink of his water.

"You really don't think Simon's involved?"

Charles glared at her. "No. But we'll, undoubtedly, know more when he's located."

"Seems no one can locate him either. Not since he flew to Ohio in October. Merek found that he flew on three commercial flights to get to Clintonville, but he can't trail him flying back to Spain. Could've hired a jet, changed his name. Who knows? Maybe taken a train around the country, then left. But Merek's checked out everything. His last whereabouts stop in Clintonville though. No record of him going back to Spain or leaving Ohio, for that matter."

Charles shifted in his chair. "I hope he's not living there."

"You wouldn't take him back? I mean, if he's not involved in any of this?"

"Most certainly not. Not at this point. What is it they say? Too little. Too late."

"Good for you. I know it's taken you a long time to get over him." She paused. "As much as I'll miss you, I think moving to Switzerland is a good idea." She faked a smile. "Oh, you …" She got up and hugged him. They held each other for several moments.

"I agree. But you must come visit. We'll go kayaking. There are some incredibly beautiful places there," he said.

"I'm sure. Stratton and I …" She turned from him. "Anyway, you want to order some lunch?"

Her iPhone rang. She knew the caller from the ringtone. She walked to the table, picked it up, and tapped the talk icon. "Hey, Merek. What's up?"

"Miss H. I got a call back from the auto shop that tinted the windows on the black truck that probably ran over you. I offered bonuses and got several callbacks, but this is the only man who described the truck grille."

"Do you know who owned the truck?"

"No, Miss H. But he said he is thirty miles from Derby Crossing. He said that a Mexican man, maybe five foot, dressed in a flannel shirt, jeans, and work boots, drove the truck in and waited for the tint to be done a few weeks ago. The owner said it would take several hours, but the man said he did not care. He would wait and he had to have it that day. They worked late into the night, and the man paid cash and drove away. No name, no address."

Emma paused in thought as Charles stood and walked over to her with a questioning look on his face. She held up an index finger signaling him to wait.

"He still have any of the cash?" she asked.

"Yes."

"And?"

"And I told him to not touch it and to take the money in a baggie to the police station and tell them why. He said he would not go to the police. So I told him that you will be by to pick up the money and give him a bonus."

"Great work, Merek."

"Thanks, Miss H... I gotta scram."

"I wasn't going to call you," Emma said to Detective Arnold as they pulled out of the hotel parking lot in Emma's pickup, "but I decided it would probably be best if I did."

"You're right about that. I've checked you out, Miss Haines. You and Joey have quite a track record for catching criminals."

"Joey. You know him?"

"I do. My territory is Ohio and surrounding states and I met him a couple of times. Cocky little jerk."

Emma laughed.

Arnold laughed. "I guess it takes one to know one is what you're thinking."

Emma looked out the windshield and didn't answer. She didn't know Arnold, but she knew to be in any role of law enforcement you had to have enough confidence in yourself to do the job and it sometimes came off as what Arnold thought of Joey. Some people thought the same thing about her, but she didn't care.

Arnold's presence filled her truck, which made her miss Stratton even more.

"So we can likely get prints off this money," he said, changing the subject.

"Don't see why not if this guy is in AFIS. Chances are he's got a sheet if he's involved in running over people and kidnapping."

"That's for sure. Sad, but true. Being a criminal is just another career."

"Gives us jobs, I guess," she said as she drove fast down the highway. She could feel Arnold staring at the side of her face. "What?" she said, glancing toward him.

He was grinning. "I really shouldn't have allowed you to come, you know. I should be handling this solo. It's my jur. You know that."

"So what are you doing here?"

He turned toward the window, the broken white lines zipping by in the side mirror as Emma passed another car.

"Because your guy found this and I know you want to find Reeves and you're smart and a good investigator. Otherwise, I'd have made you stay at the hotel."

"Made me? Do you think I would've stayed at the hotel?"

He gave her a look. "I could've had you … detained." He looked out his side window. She didn't answer.

They traveled in silence for some time before he continued, "I know it's not an appropriate situation to say this, but I find you very attractive and enjoy your company. You've been on my mind. Guess that's another reason why we're here."

"Ahh. Well, I'm sure a man like you has his share of women."

"Funny you say that. Man like me has not been on a successful date in over two years. Not quite a share, in my terms."

"And how do you define successful?" she asked.

He chuckled. "It's not what you're thinking. I define a successful date as being one where I want to see the woman again.

Down to earth. Same interests. Smart. Attractive. The spark. You know."

Her ears turned red before she said, "And you've been on unsuccessful dates for over two years? I'm surprised."

"About six times. That's only about three a year. My job keeps me busy, and I have two ex-wives and three kids." He paused. "I think you have many of the qualities I mentioned, Emma." He looked out the window.

She ignored his comment. After several moments she said, "Wow. Guess you are busy."

"You don't have kids and never married."

She glanced at him and smiled. Of course, he would know everything about her. "Never was that interested in either one. I decided to marry my job."

"But then you met Stratton Reeves. He wrote a story in his paper about that Calhoon character. And then he was shot in Chillicothe. While he was with you."

Her jaw tightened, but she said nothing. "Anyway, I read a lot of his columns. Won lots of writing awards, I understand. He was a great writer."

"Don't you mean *is* a great writer?"

Arnold looked at the floorboard.

Her iPhone map informed them the destination was a mile ahead. "We'll be at the auto shop in a few minutes. You may want to let me do the talking, okay? Once he sees you and you tell him you're FBI, he'll probably freak out. From what Merek told me, he wouldn't have anything to do with the police station.

I'm guessing he gets a lot of cash business in these parts that the IRS doesn't know about, or he's had a run-in with the law or all of the above. I didn't have time to check him out before I left.

"I'm sure you're armed, right?"

Chapter II

"HE's A FINE Thoroughbred, Mr. Smith. He'll win you a lot of money in Spain," Fred Denver said.

Dayton Kotmister walked around King's Runner, sliding his hands over the animal and patting him. "He is beautiful and has a fine record. I've wanted to own him for years," Kotmister said.

The horse whinnied. His huge brown eyes took in the sights as he stood inside the barn in a set of cross-ties hooked to either side of his halter. He pawed at the ground, snorted, and bounced his head.

"I'll have the money wired to your account within the hour," Kotmister said as he came around to stand in front of the horse, petting his nose.

"That's fine. I can deliver him to the airport in the morning, then. When did you say your plane would be there?"

"Five. I've hired the best stock plane for his comfort. He will live like a king," Kotmister said. "Like a king." He kissed the horse's nose. The horse jerked his head away. "You will love it in the mountain fields."

Fred had never been paid this much for any horse in his fifty years in the business. His ship had come in when Mr. Smith's
associate had met with him last October. He really didn't want
to sell the horse, but the offer was too much to refuse. Odd
birds, Mr. Smith and his associate. But Fred didn't care. If the
five million came through as this so-called Mr. Smith prom-
ised, he didn't care if he went by Santa Claus. His money would
spend like anyone else's.

"Thank you, Mr. Denver," Kotmister said. They shook
hands. "I assure you this horse will be living on the finest estate."

"Sounds good. I'll see you in the morning."

"Don't be late," Kotmister said before he strolled out of the
barn and slid into the Camry.

He shifted the car into drive, and it crept along the paved
drive to the main road away from the Denver Horse Farm.
Once on the main highway, Kotmister punched the gas. *How
I miss my Ferrari.*

His visit to the United States was paying off in many ways.
The ransom for Stratton Reeves, who was now going to write
his life story, had helped pay for a horse he always wanted to
own. And he killed Emma Haines—the one person who nearly
ruined it all for him.

Kotmister slowed to the speed limit on the highway. "I'm
a genius," he yelled as he hit the steering wheel with his hands.
"I must celebrate."

He pulled into the Spanish restaurant around seven and asked
for a table in the back. No one seemed to notice him as he

strolled through several tables full of people eating and talking, many of them speaking Spanish.

Poncio greeted him, but he learned not to try and be friendly with this man. Hopefully, he would tip as much as he had before.

"You will have a glass of Pingus?" Poncio asked, meekly.

"Make it a bottle. I have much to celebrate," Dayton answered in Spanish.

"That is wonderful. I will be right back with it."

Kotmister pulled off his leather gloves and placed them on the table before he sat down, his back against the wall so he could watch the customers. He pulled his cellphone from his jacket pocket and tapped the front before he held it to his ear.

"Come and celebrate with me. I have closed the deal on King's Runner and I do not want to celebrate alone. Meet me here at the Spanish restaurant I told you about. Mr. Reeves will be fine alone for a few hours. He cannot escape." He ended the call and laid the iPhone on the table.

Poncio came from around the side of the table, poured the wine, and told him about the Wednesday evening specials.

Dayton picked up his wine glass and examined the dark liquid through the light. It was their third bottle after several cocktails.

"Oh, and look at this," Dayton slurred, pulling out his iPhone. He hit the Facebook icon, tapped the screen, and held it toward José, who examined it. "A Facebook memorial page for the late Emma Haines. She's dead." They laughed as Dayton slid the phone back into his pocket.

"Let's get back. I need to rest. Runner will be delivered to the airport at five in the morning when the plane arrives. We will load him and leave quickly."

"Big plane, little airport. How did you do it?" José asked.

"Oh, my friend. People will do anything for money. You know that." Dayton said, draining his full glass of wine.

"*Sí.*"

Dayton snapped his fingers and motioned toward Poncio to bring the check. He paid for their dinner with cash and left a sixty percent tip. The men laughed and talked as they weaved their way through the restaurant and parking lot toward their vehicles.

"And how was our guest doing when you left?"

"He was sleeping on the couch."

"I believe he'll love Spain, don't you? Oh, it will be glorious to get back home and have a book written about me."

"*Sí.* I do not like America."

"That's what I've always liked about you, José. We think alike," Kotmister said, patting José on the back.

José nodded. "I will see you in the morning." They parted ways walking toward their cars.

Dayton got into the Camry, and José slid behind the wheel of the Honda parked a few spaces away. He followed Dayton as they pulled out of the parking lot.

Dayton glanced in the rearview mirror at José's headlights. He needed him to guard Stratton until they got to his estate. When he told José's brother how much he was going to pay him to kill José, the deal was made. *People will do anything for money. Even kill their own brother.* He smiled.

His mind shifted as he pictured his book in stores and on bookshelves in many languages. *Who wouldn't want to read about me?* And he would make appearances all over the world to promote his book, written by his famous—deceased—friend Stratton Reeves, killed in a tragic accident soon after the book was finished. Another job for José's brother.

They got out of their cars at the ranch and Dayton walked over to one of the pasture fences where a horse stood watching them. José said good night and headed toward the house.

"We had a good ride this morning, didn't we? Yes. Yes," Dayton cooed to the horse, patting its neck. "Such a shame I will have to say goodbye to my old friend when we get home. But we do what we must in this world, don't we?" He stroked the horse's neck and the horse snorted and bumped Dayton's shoulder with its nose.

"That's right. I may even miss him for a little while."

The horse bobbed its head and sputtered.

"That's right. Yes. That's right."

The horse nudged him, and Dayton cackled toward the moon.

"Czesc."

Silence.

"Are you there?"

Finally the woman's voice said, "Merek."

"Tak. Jak si masz?"

Silence.

"I am okay. Why are you calling me after six months?" Ludnella asked.

Merek rubbed his hand over his face.

"I wondered how you are doing."

She drew in a deep breath and let it out slowly. "I am doing fine, considering."

"Considering what?"

She didn't answer.

He sat back on his leather sofa. "I have been thinking."

"About?"

"About you. About us. About how we were."

"We were fine until you chose Emma Haines. You chose her over me."

He frowned. "I had to stay. She made me partner."

"You chose her over me! You love her more than anyone."

"*Nie.* As a boss and friend, not a lover."

"She is your boss, so true. Jump, Merek. How high, Miss H.?" she said in a mocking voice. "Look, I have to get to work."

"Where do you work?"

"I'm a waitress at a high class restaurant. I make good money."

"That is good."

"I have to go, Merek."

"Wait."

"What do you want?"

He stood. "I want to come there. Stay with you, say a week or two weeks. See what happens, then maybe—"

"Maybe? Maybe what? You'll take me back? You will choose me over Emma Haines? Then I am supposed to kiss you and make up? Maybe that? You chose her. Not me!"

"No. It is not like that. She is my partner. I never chose her over you. You left me. You went to Colorado. You could have stayed here with me. I could have given you a good life. You do not understand."

"I understand one thing. I married a man who chose me. He chose me."

Merek dropped onto the couch.

"You are married? Already? Who is this man?"

"You stay in Ohio, Merek Polanski, with your Emma Haines and your *partnership* and your money."

The call went dead.

Merek rode his Harley out of the underground parking garage and merged onto highway 315 North.

Maybe Ludnella had a point. He had chosen Emma over her in a way. But to be a full partner in a business was a dream come true for him. And she left him. She could've stayed with him. He didn't want to go to Colorado. He had a good job here, and he loved living in Clintonville.

When he called his parents back in Poland, they were ecstatic about him working for Emma. Then when he called them and told them she made him full partner in the business, they were happy beyond words. His father was so proud he just kept saying, *"Jestem bardzo dumny,"* over and over. "I am very proud."

His mother cried so hard with joy that she couldn't even talk to him.

And he was proud, too. Emma paid him more money in a month than he ever dreamed he could make in his entire life. In Poland, he would probably still be looking for work, even with his degree in computer science from the *Uniwersytet Warszawski*.

He could have any woman he wanted, and he could afford to buy anything. Any woman, that is, until Ludnella. Oddly, he hadn't realized how much he cared about her until he started seeing Fantasy. He frequented the gentlemen's club and shoved a lot of money down G-strings. Lately, Fantasy had been the dancer waking up in his bed. But every time he was with her, he missed Ludnella.

I have come here and I live the American Dream. Why am I not happy?

As his Harley hit ninety miles per hour, an SUV cut in front of him and he swerved. He braked hard as the car's rear bumper hit his front tire. His bike wobbled and the obscenities bounced off the face cover of his motorcycle helmet before he merged over into the right lane and slowed to the legal speed.

He rode up Hog Back Road and pulled over. He got off the bike, removed his helmet, and looked out over the north end of Alum Creek. The sun hung low in the sky. The smell of fish, dirt, water, and pine from a nearby stand of evergreens was in the evening air.

Osprey settled in on their nesting platforms, calling and squawking to one another, likely sitting on eggs or chicks.

He unzipped his leather jacket and pulled out his Samsung, swiping screens, checking texts, email, and his Facebook page. Nothing from Emma, and nothing else he cared to read.

Maybe he should go back to Kentucky. But what could he do there that he couldn't do here with Joey? And he wanted to be home in his apartment to think and to be alone. Away from people. He slipped his phone back into the inside jacket pocket and looked out over the water.

An osprey screamed, followed by many sharp squawks and calls from other birds.

"You call. You fly free. You eat fish. Do you ever get tired of fish?" he yelled toward the birds.

As if replying, another bird called out.

"You live to take care of your babies. Then they fly away. That's what you do without question."

The birds screeched and squawked.

He gazed at the sky and took another deep breath. Spring. The time for new beginnings.

The trees around him were about to unfurl their small green leaves from bursting buds and wildflowers spotted the hills through the woods. Emma had told him about this place. She kayaked here. She and Charles, and now, she and Stratton. *Poor Mr. Stratton.* His mind switched to *New York Natalie* smiling at him and leaning against the old counter in the store. For a split second he could nearly smell her perfume. "NYN," he whispered.

"I do need to go back to Poland to see my parents. I flew away, but I must fly back. I should be in my homeland and take care of them."

His mother had raised three boys. His two younger brothers had also gone to college, but they were working in jobs that paid low wages in Poland. They weren't happy when Merek left them to pursue his dreams in America. But Merek had asked them to join him, and they refused. They had many excuses, but he knew they were afraid.

He understood, remembering the feeling of stepping onto the plane that would take him to another world in a matter of hours. He nearly turned and ran back down the walkway into the airport, but instead had smiled at the pretty flight attendant, found his seat, and buckled up. He never flew before and had saved his money from working in a grocery to buy his plane ticket.

He had wanted to go to America. He wanted to go to The Ohio State University and become a Buckeye since he saw the article and pictures in a magazine at the grocery. He wanted to learn to play an instrument and be in The Best Damn Band in the Land, also known as TBDBITL. He worked with an American friend at the grocery who taught Merek to speak English quite well. He was sharp—a quick learner.

As soon as he arrived in America, he landed a job at a small computer store in Clintonville. He loved it and felt he was rich. Then in walked Emma Haines to buy a laptop, and she asked him to be her assistant. They walked out of the store together, and the rest was history.

He looked at the back of the motorcycle seat where Ludnella and Fantasy and many other women had held him around the waist. They kissed his neck or nibbled his ears as they soared over the roads like free birds on their way to a cozy nest.

"Is this freedom? Is this life in America? Is this it?" he yelled in Polish at the sunset.

An osprey screeched.

"I will take that as a yes, my bird friend. Goodbye."

He put his helmet on, threw his leg over the seat, and started the engine.

His phone vibrated as he rode. He would check it at the Wildflower Café while he was eating the sautéed pork schnitzel.

"We'll get the fingerprints off these bills as soon as we get to the police station and run it through the database. It's late, but I called someone and they'll be there," Arnold said, holding up the plastic baggie, which held seventy dollars—supposedly the cash left from the business transaction.

"How long?" Emma asked.

"Pretty quick," Arnold said, leaning back in the passenger seat of Emma's truck. They went down the highway for some time, lost in their thoughts until Arnold broke the silence. "I can't imagine what you're going through, Miss Haines. Something like this happen to someone I love, hard to tell what I'd do. I'm truly sorry."

She didn't answer. They rode in silence to the police station. They got out of the truck and went in.

"I'll run this down to the lab," he said.

"I'll wait in the conference room."

He turned away, and she walked into the conference room and sat down. She propped her chin in her hands, reading the names on the board, focusing on the upper corner with a big red circle around the name Dayton Kotmister. It had been too long for Emma to remember his voice.

She dug her iPad out of her Fossil purse and connected to the station's guest Wi-Fi. She had a Facebook message: *I am a waiter here and see the man in picture on our page two times. He was here tonight with another man. I'm at work now and can talk to you. Poncio.* The time stamp was ten minutes prior.

Her heart beat in her ears and she ran down the hall to the lab. She pounded on the door and Arnold opened it.

"We don't have a match yet, but it shouldn't be but a minute. What's wrong?"

"We have to go. Now! Dayton Kotmister ate dinner at a Spanish restaurant not far from here tonight and someone there wants to talk to me right now."

"You got it." He turned to a lab worker in a white jacket. "Call me as soon as you find anything." The lab technician nodded and waved.

Emma and Arnold ran down the hall and out the door of the police station, Arnold jabbering on his Bluetooth.

"We got a match on the prints. Spanish mobster who uses many names."

"We're here to see Poncio," Arnold said, flashing his badge at the host. He looked terrified and wasted no time finding the waiter.

A small Spanish boy who might have been pushing sixteen peeked around the corner. Emma waved at him. "Poncio?"

He turned his attention toward Arnold, who was walking toward him. Emma held Arnold's arm. "Stay here," she whispered.

"Poncio, I'm Emma Haines and this is my friend, Agent Arnold."

"No policía. No. No policía." Poncio whispered through his teeth before he turned and took off running.

Arnold and Emma ran after him, chasing him through the swinging doors of the restaurant and through the kitchen of people cooking in white shirts and black and white striped pants. Pots and pans clanked loudly as they hit the floor when Arnold shoved two workers aside, apologizing. Emma jumped over the pots like a gazelle as Arnold led the chase.

Arnold quickly caught up to Poncio in the parking lot. "We're not going to hurt you, we just want to talk to you about your Facebook message you sent to Miss Haines," Arnold yelled.

Poncio looked around like a wild animal ready to run. Emma thought of Earl Calhoon when they hit the Grassy Shoals boat ramp last October on the New River. He frantically looked for an outhouse that had been torn down where he stashed a stolen necklace forty years earlier.

"You're scaring him," Emma said in a low voice as she came up behind Arnold.

"No doubt."

"Poncio, we're not here about you, we're here about the man you sent me a note about. That's all. That's it. We don't care about you. It's okay. We're not going to take you anywhere.

We're not here for you. But you can help save someone's life if you talk to us about the man you've seen here. Please, Poncio. You'll get money, a reward, for talking to us. You will. Will you help us?" Emma asked.

Poncio stood in the parking lot, looking like he was about to cry.

"We just want to talk to you about the man at the restaurant," Emma said, slowly approaching him.

"Why don't we go back inside and sit down? I'd like a cup of coffee. Can we talk over a cup of coffee?"

"*Sí.*"

"Let's go back in. Come on." Emma slowly turned and walked toward Arnold and the restaurant. She motioned with her eyes for him to follow. Her insides were shaking so hard she thought she might rattle apart. *Calm. Stay calm.* Poncio finally followed them back into the restaurant.

The three of them sat in a booth and a waitress brought their coffee. Emma and Arnold thanked her. The waitress bowed, staring at Poncio before she scurried away.

Poncio's eyes were glued to the table, his hands wrapped tightly around his coffee mug.

"It was very kind of you to send the message about the man to me. Thank you for coming back in to talk to us," Emma said as calmly as she could to the black curly crown of Poncio's head. "I appreciate anything you can tell me about him. It's very important."

Poncio slowly raised his head and examined their faces before he finally said, "He tip big cash."

"That's great, right?" Arnold said with a huge smile.

"*Sí*. Good."

"What else can you tell us about him?"

Poncio dropped his gaze to the table again. Emma reached out and touched his arm.

"Poncio, please. My boyfriend is in danger and the man you waited on could help me find him. Do you understand?"

He nodded slowly. "*Sí*."

"Please help me, Poncio," Emma begged.

Poncio nodded and finally raised his head.

"Man come in yesterday for lunch. He speak in Spanish. I try to make friendly talk with him. But he mean. But he leave big tip. Then he come back tonight. Then another man join him. They sit back there in back of restaurant." He paused. "I hear things and tonight, he talk nice to me. He was very happy. The men were celebrating. Drank a lot."

"What did they say, Poncio?" Arnold asked.

"Man say he just bought horse."

"He bought a horse?" Emma asked.

"*Sí*. King's something. I do not hear everything."

"Anything else?" Arnold asked.

"Man on phone say Mr. Reese cannot escape."

Emma clenched her fists under the table. "Mr. Reese? Could it have been Mr. Reeves?" she asked slowly.

Poncio shrugged. "*Sí*. Maybe."

"I knew he was still alive," she whispered, pulling her iPhone out of her purse, shaking. She tried to do several Google searches, frowned, and shook her head. She hit the speed icon for Merek.

"Did the men say where they were staying? Where they bought the horse?" Arnold asked.

Poncio shook his head. "That is all I hear."

Chapter 12

MEREK LISTENED TO Fantasy's voice mail again.

"I'm sorry. Please come by tonight. We'll talk things through. Please call me as soon as you get this. We have a really good thing, baby. Don't blow it."

He sat on his couch and tossed his cell on the glass and chrome coffee table. He picked up the remote, pointed it at the 70-inch Samsung hanging on the wall, and flipped through the channels. He finally landed on a Cleveland Indians baseball game.

He put the remote on the table, got up, walked into his kitchen, reached into his Bosch fridge, and pulled out a *Zywiec* he bought at Weiland's Market. He opened the Polish beer, tossed the lid in the trash, and took a long swig as he walked through the living room and into his bedroom. He placed the beer on a coaster on his dresser, took off his clothes, and threw them in the hamper. He pulled on his Japanese red silk robe and went back into the living room, sipping his beer. He set the beer down and stretched out on the couch.

His phone chimed. It was Emma. He took it from the table and hit the speaker icon.

"Hey, Miss H."

"We may be able to nail Kotmister, but I need your help. Now."

He sat at attention and picked up a tablet and pen, *"Jasna cholera.* Go."

"I need you to find a horse sales transaction for a fast Thoroughbred around the Derby Crossing area. The horse's name begins with King or Kings, but that's all I know." She proceeded to tell him about talking with Poncio. "Kotmister bought this horse, so we have to track it down. Stratton's life depends on it."

"Right. I gotta scram."

He took a fast swig of beer. He ran, carrying the beer and his phone into his office. The walls were covered with pictures of Poland he framed in designer silver and gold frames. A large picture of Brutus Buckeye, the mascot for The Ohio State University, hung on another wall, along with pictures of several of the college's football players. He glanced at a picture of his parents smiling proudly into the camera beside a picture of Mother Mary. "Send me strength," he whispered in Polish as he hit the mouse, bringing his sleeping laptop to life.

A loud pounding on his apartment door interrupted his research. *"Gówno!"* He slapped his desk, jumped from his chair, and ran to the door while he tightened his robe sash. He looked through the peephole and put his head against the door. He sighed and opened it.

"You going to invite me in?" Fantasy asked.

He stood, blocking her, leaning against the door, his arms crossed in front of his chest.

"I cannot. I am working."

She eyed him. "I'll bet. Who is she?" She pushed past him and ran through his condo and into the bedroom. Merek closed the door behind him.

She walked back into the living room her head down, smiling, with her hands behind her back. "What are you working on? It's late," she asked in almost a whisper.

"You must go. Now."

She walked through the room and sat down on the couch. She dropped her head in her hands. She raised her head and said, "I knew you wouldn't cheat on me." She walked over to him, put her arms around his neck, and tried to kiss him. He took her arms off him and gently pushed her away.

"You need to leave. I am working."

"Okay. I'll cook you something to eat while you work." She walked toward the kitchen.

"No. Go."

"I'll just sit out here until you're finished." She stopped. "Then I'll help you relax." She winked at him.

He opened the door. "You must leave. Now."

"But—"

"Now."

She stomped to the door and stood in the doorway. "Call me later."

He gently pushed her out into the hallway and shut the door in her face.

Emma and Agent Arnold sat in the conference room at the Derby Crossing police station. She was on her iPad and Arnold was talking with a police officer.

"We've interviewed most of the horse farm owners within a ten mile radius of here, but I just don't have the manpower to keep this up. I'm sorry," the officer said to Arnold. "We've come up with nothing. We're doing all we can."

"I understand," Arnold replied. "But we need to find who sold that horse." He turned and walked over to the table and sat down opposite Emma.

"I've got Jay and my men in Washington on this, making calls. We've got it covered."

Emma didn't glance up from her iPad.

"I've got everyone I can working hard on this," he said.

She ignored him.

He leaned back and straightened his black tie, pressing it down his white shirt. "Hey, look, it's getting late and I'm starved. Would you like to get a bite?"

"No, thanks. Charles and I are getting room service at the hotel," she answered, not looking up. Seconds after she said it, Charles strutted through the door looking as if he just left a photo shoot for men's designer clothing.

"Any news on the location of the horse owner?" he asked as he sat in a chair next to Emma.

She looked him up and down and shook her head. "No. I found a horse named King, but when I called the farm, they said they still owned it and it wasn't for sale. Locals here went out and talked to him. Seems straight. Merek's working on it, too."

"This is an FBI matter," Arnold snapped.

She ignored him.

Charles said, "Let's go get something to eat. I'm famished."

Arnold stood and looked down at the top of Emma's head. "I'll contact you as soon as I hear anything, Miss Haines. Try and get some rest after you eat your room service meal." He gave Charles a look and left.

Emma glared at his back as he walked out of the room.

"What is going on here?" Charles made a back and forth motion with a finger, pointing to Emma and the doorway.

"What do you mean?" she said, not looking up from her iPad.

"You can cut the tension between you two with a knife, that's what I mean. And it's not good, Emma. You don't want to anger the FBI. They're doing all they can, and it is in their jurisdiction. They can arrest you, you know."

"Merek found the money, not them. It was my post that the waiter replied to, not theirs. No one's going to contact the FBI and have a friendly chat. Come on. Really? And I doubt they bothered with posts on restaurant pages anyway." She gave an angry nod toward the door.

Charles sat back and stretched his legs in front of him, crossing his ankles. He wore tasseled loafers, purple socks, a perfectly creased pair of purple khakis, and a starched white shirt.

"Going out?" she asked.

"Yes. And you're coming with me. We need to take a rest from all this. Staying cooped up here and in the hotel is making us both much too stressed. Between this and Mary, I need a small break." He fiddled with his gray mustache.

She shook her head. "It's late. I'm going back to the hotel and order a pizza. I'm beat."

"No, you're not going to the hotel, eat a frozen pizza, go to bed, and be awake the entire night. We're going to have a lovely dinner at The Grovebrook. It's just down the street so we won't be far. I telephoned, and their kitchen is open until one. I've heard it's lovely—delicious food, live piano and jazz music. Oh, my." He turned to the whiteboard and focused on Simon's name. "Yes. That's right. Oh, dear. It was Simon who told me about that restaurant." He stood and walked to the whiteboard.

"Simon?" Emma jumped up and followed him.

"Yes, I just remembered. He was there on business. Why had I not remembered this?"

"Business? Here? Like investments? Horses? What?"

He shook his head. "I would assume it was for his consulting firm. I really don't know. But I just remembered he mentioned going to The Grovebrook."

"Do you remember who he was meeting? Who he was with? Kotmister's friends or something? Think!"

Charles frowned, tapping his chin in thought as he took several steps in a circle. "I don't know, but it was shortly before he left."

"Before he left to go to Spain?" Emma's eyes followed Charles's to Simon's name on the whiteboard and the thick black line to Kotmister's name in the red circle.

Her cell buzzed and she ran to the table, picked it up, tapped it, and held it to her ear.

"What do ya got, Merek?" She sat down and pulled her notebook from her purse and scribbled in it.

"Yes. Yes. Got it. Awesome work. Right. Right."

Charles jogged back to the table. "What did he discover?"

"King's Runner. Let's go."

"What are you doing here, Miss Haines?" Agent Jay said as he and Agent Arnold went to her. "And you, Mr. Wellington?"

Neither of them answered as she and Charles walked over the rise on a gravel drive leading to a horse barn. Bugs flitted around a large outdoor light hanging over the doorway. A man wearing a dirty pair of bib overalls stood under the light, leaning on a pitchfork. She jogged toward him, her brunette ponytail bouncing below her ball cap. Charles, Arnold, and Jay followed closely behind.

"Hello, sir. My name is Emma Haines and this is FBI agents Arnold and Jay, and my friend, Charles Wellington."

"We need to speak with the owner of King's Runner," Arnold jumped in.

The man looked shocked. "FBI? What is this?"

Arnold and Jay stepped up to the man and showed him their badges. "We're investigating a kidnapping and need to ask you a few questions."

The man froze. His eyes moved back and forth. He shifted his weight from one foot to the other.

"Kidnapping?"

"You sell a horse named King's Runner recently?"

"Yes, I sold him earlier today, as a matter of fact. Why?"

"To this man?" Arnold showed him a picture of Dayton Kotmister on his iPhone.

"Yes, that's the man. Mr. Smith. Why, what's the problem? Has he been kidnapped?"

"Mr. Smith. He couldn't do any better than that?" Emma nearly shrieked. Arnold gave her a look.

"Your name, please, sir," Jay said.

"Fred Denver. This is my place. What's this about?"

"Mr. Smith isn't Mr. Smith. His name is Dayton Kotmister, and we need to locate him immediately. Do you know how we can locate him?"

Denver inhaled deeply, picturing his millions disintegrating into the air. He felt like he might throw up. He already put a down payment on the mansion in Florida after Smith's money hit his account. He closed his eyes. "I'm to deliver King's Runner to the county airport in the morning. He's having a plane come and take the horse to Spain."

"What time?" Emma asked.

"Five."

"You don't know where he is now?" Jay asked.

Denver shook his head. "He wired the money for the horse to my account. He didn't tell me where he was staying. I didn't ask. That's all I know. I never met the man before in my life. I swear."

"How did he come to buy the horse, then? Just show up? Was it listed for sale?" Emma asked.

Denver shrugged. "He called a couple weeks ago. Said he sent someone in October to look him over and gave me an offer."

"And who was here in October?" Arnold asked.

"Man named Beara."

"José Beara." Arnold said.

Emma glanced at Arnold. "Kotmister's sidekick," she said. Arnold nodded.

"We'll need you to come with us, Mr. Denver," Jay said. Arnold turned, talking into his Bluetooth.

"I suppose I'll have to give the money back," Mr. Denver said.

"You have no sale," Agent Jay said.

Denver leaned on the pitchfork and dropped his head.

Emma turned and walked toward her truck. "You're way out of line here, Miss Haines. You know that," Arnold said, jogging up beside her.

She gave him an icy look.

"No buts. Ours. You stay OUT. Am I clear on this? Go back to the hotel then back to Ohio, or I'll have you arrested."

She marched past him to her truck, climbed in the driver's side, and slammed the door.

It was three-thirty in the morning when Stratton had walked into the living room from his bedroom. He looked up at the mirrors, betting that José and Dayton would sleep in as late as possible—with hangovers. He heard a car leave in the afternoon and suspected it was Dayton's. He heard another leave early in the evening and figured it was José. He heard them both return around midnight and the elevator going to the top floor.

He took the mixture of wine and ketchup he made while the men were out and covered the carpet and the corner of the glass tabletop in front of the couch. He put a dab of the mixture on the side of his head and a streak down his forehead. He got down on the floor, put his head in the stained carpet, and waited. No matter what—he was not getting on that plane in less than two hours. He had to escape—or he'd die trying.

He was still trying to breathe slowly, not move, stay awake, and listen to every sound. After what seemed like a lifetime, the metal door opened and closed. Footsteps. Not Dayton's. He didn't know how large José was, but at this point it didn't matter.

Stratton felt someone standing next to him, and he peeked through his eye next to the carpet. A pair of worn work boots, average size, with frayed jeans hanging over them were about a foot from his head. As the boots circled him, Stratton reached out, grabbed the man's ankles, and jerked hard.

José went down with a thud and a grunt. Stratton scrambled on top of him and punched José in the face several times. He grabbed the rifle and got to his feet.

José lay on the carpet panting, holding his jaw, looking up at Stratton with large bloodshot eyes. He obviously lied about not knowing the door codes.

"Don't move or I'll put the little red dot on *you* for a change. I won't miss, either." Stratton sneered, aiming the gun at José's chest.

"*Señor.* Don't shoot. Don't shoot. I came to see if you were hurt. That is all. I saw you, and I was worried. We have become good friends and I worry," he said in a squeaky voice, smiling, rubbing his jaw. Sweat ran down his brow.

"If you've got a cellphone, hand it over. Now."

José shook his head. "I have no phone."

"Get up. Spread your legs, fingers weaved behind your head."

José stood as he was told. Stratton bumped his legs farther apart and did a quick pat-down. No phone. "Let's go."

José got to his feet and plodded toward the door when the sound of the elevator started.

"Quick! In the bedroom." He motioned with the rifle, and José walked slowly toward Stratton's bedroom. When José opened the door, Stratton hit him in the back of the head with the butt of the gun. José went down and appeared to be out cold on the floor.

Stratton shut the door and wedged a chair under the handle. It would have to do.

He jogged over to the wall behind the gray metal door and pressed his back against it. He checked the rifle again. It had been over forty years since he fired one, in a jungle. His eyes fixed on the crack of the door. Sweat formed on his upper lip and forehead. His vision blurred. He blinked.

José slammed against the bedroom door, and Stratton jerked his head up. "Damn," he whispered under his breath as the gray metal door opened.

Stratton inhaled and leaned back. Dayton Kotmister's back appeared in front of him as the door shut and clicked.

He inhaled, raised the rifle, and aimed. The red laser dot appeared on Dayton's back. "Don't move, Kotmister."

Dayton stopped. He turned slowly and cocked his head. Stratton raised the rifle, and the red dot appeared between Dayton's eyes.

Dayton grinned.

Stratton wrapped his right index finger around the trigger.

"Now, Mr. Reeves. What do you think you're doing? We've got a plane to catch."

"No plane. We're leaving, and I'm taking you in."

Dayton chuckled. "Really?"

"Really. Let's go." Stratton motioned with the rifle. You're going to key the codes into the doors, open them, and stay in front of me at all times."

Dayton didn't budge.

Stratton aimed the laser at Dayton's knee and motioned with the rifle. "Move!"

Dayton slowly walked past him toward the door. He put his hand on the door handle, leaned into the door, and in one fluid movement, turned and kicked the rifle up.

The gun went off, and a bullet shattered the ceiling. Plaster fell to the floor, and the sound of the shot echoed through the room like a cannon. José screamed something in Spanish.

Another kick, and Stratton fell on the floor. The rifle popped out of his hand and landed on the carpet near the fake bloodstain. Dayton screamed as he jumped on Stratton like a wild animal.

Stratton scrambled backward on the floor. He tried pushing and kneeing Dayton off him, but Dayton was younger and faster and, obviously, knew martial arts.

Dayton's long bony fingers went around Stratton's neck and squeezed. Stratton clawed them away and rocked hard, throwing Dayton to the left of him. Stratton found his feet and went for the rifle.

Dayton ran toward the gray door, tapping at the keypad. Stratton wasn't going to get the rifle in time to stop him. Dayton twisted the handle and cracked the door open just as Stratton rammed him against it like a linebacker. Dayton's body slammed between the door and Stratton. He let out a yelp and a moan, turning toward Stratton.

Stratton punched him hard in the face, and his head snapped back and bounced off the door. Blood flew from Dayton's nose and lips. Dayton's eyes went crazy, and he growled and screamed.

Stratton stepped back to throw another punch, but Dayton chopped him in the throat and the sides of his neck. Stratton went down. He crawled up the wall with his hands, stood, and turned. The barrel of the rifle was a foot from his face.

"Oh, Mr. Reeves. I really wish you hadn't done this."

Chapter 13

"YOU SHOULDN'T HAVE lied to the FBI, Emma," Charles said.

"I didn't lie. They know we're here."

Charles shook his head. "We shouldn't be here. And we're not armed."

"They're armed." She sipped her coffee.

"We've been here since three in the morning, sitting in this cold pickup truck in the woods along a county airport runway in Derby Crossing, Kentucky."

"Did you ever think you'd have so much fun when you met me?" she asked, not taking her eyes from the windshield.

"Fun. Right. I've been shot at in West Virginia, nearly shot at in Ohio, and now this."

"You haven't been shot at here."

Charles put both palms to the air. "Yet!"

"So why'd you agree to come with me? You could've stayed at the hotel."

"Oh, Emma. Really."

She reached over and patted his arm. "Thank you. I appreciate it."

"This is, frankly, outrageous. You never leave the authorities alone. You're always butting in. It's just not proper. I believe you've gone crazy." He crossed his arms in front of his chest and sulked.

She checked the clock on her truck—four forty-five. "You save spaceships from crashing into Earth and you call me crazy?" she said, looking up for plane lights.

"It's my job. This is not your job. That's the difference."

"If Kotmister had kidnapped me, I know you'd be sitting here."

Charles didn't reply.

"Look," she pointed out the windshield.

A plane's lights blinked as they lowered, approaching the runway.

"The plane to Spain," she whispered. As it landed, Fred Denver's truck and horse trailer pulled in along the other side of the runway.

Denver got out of his truck as a black Toyota Camry pulled in behind it and Kotmister emerged from the passenger side.

"There he is," she whispered.

Kotmister looked around before he walked toward Denver. They shook hands and walked to the horse trailer, Kotmister following with his head down and his hands in his pockets.

"I remember that walk. I wonder if he bleached his hair while he was in prison," she said.

Denver opened the back of the trailer. A beautiful chestnut horse backed out and pranced on the end of a long lead rope that Denver held. Kotmister went over and patted the horse on the neck.

A large cargo door opened in the rear of the plane as Denver and Kotmister led the animal toward it. A short man opened the passenger side door of the Camry and went to the back passenger side door. He opened it, and Stratton's head appeared above the roof.

Emma shrieked. Charles grasped her arm.

Out of the woods, SWAT officers, Arnold, Jay, sheriffs, and Joey Reed materialized as if they were mist, all pointing guns at Kotmister and the other man. Squad cars sped around the vehicles and the plane. The short man ran into the woods. Two K9 units unleashed their barking dogs, and they bolted after José.

Kotmister stopped on the runway and held his hands in the air, yelling toward Denver as he ran with the horse toward the trailer. Arnold and Jay ran out onto the runway.

Emma slowly opened her door and crept out of the woods. Charles followed.

She walked past Joey and Agent Jay and stood behind Kotmister, who had his chin on his chest while he was being cuffed. "And this time I show up to your surprise."

He whirled around and fell to the ground on his knees, shaking his head, wide-eyed. His face was cut, swollen, and bruised. "You're dead. I ran over you. I killed you. I saw you dead in the road. I saw the Facebook page," he said through swollen lips.

"You didn't kill me. You just pissed me off. Again."

Arnold helped Kotmister to his feet and walked him toward the Mercury, giving Emma a look as he passed, but saying nothing.

Stratton leaned against the hood of the Camry as the EMT removed the duct tape from his wrists. He looked up, and his mouth dropped open.

Emma ran to him and threw her arms around him. She kissed him all over his face. He pulled her close and buried his face in her neck as they sobbed.

Chapter 14

JOHN SKIMMED THE headlines of the May 5, 2012, *Circleville Herald*. "Mary, I don't understand why you're putting all this time and money into a wedding to simply have the groom arrested at the altar. Do you really want to go through with this? Why not just have him arrested now?"

They sat at the large oak kitchen table in Mary's dining room. Wedding books and bride magazines were strewn over the table. Mary had her nose buried in a thick book of table settings.

"What about this for the table decorations?"

"Did you hear what I said?"

"Yes, I did. I'm going through with this. I want this to be the biggest party ever, after they haul that man away. Everyone attending will never forget it. The press will have a grand time. And I'll be the one to have stopped him. Perfect. Just as I planned. But in a different way."

John shook his head and snapped the paper's pages. "We can have a grand outdoor summer party instead of a wedding without a bride and groom."

"We will have other parties, but none as memorable as this." Mary's eyes sparkled as much as her four carat engagement ring. "This will be an event like no other.

"You know, when Charles was younger, I dreamed of planning his wedding. Him bringing home a beautiful bride who I would take under my wing. Teach her how to play golf. Go shopping. Get massages and pedicures together. I would spoil them and their grandchildren who would call me Nana." She leaned in toward the table. "I always liked that—Nana. But life doesn't turn out the way of our dreams, does it?"

"Charles could still get married and adopt," John said.

"True. At least the chances of him marrying Simon Johnson are over. I truly despise that man. He ruined my son's life. Charles was never the same after Simon walked out on him. His eyes lost their shine. He killed a part of my son, and I will never forgive him for that. And Simon may be involved in Stratton's kidnapping. Terrible. When they find him, I hope he's put away forever."

"Yes, it's sad. People break up and always take a piece of the other person with them, usually without knowing or often caring. We're all pieces of others, I suppose. But I must say, I'm as happy about you not marrying Devereux as you are about Charles not marrying Simon."

She looked at John and felt a warmth in her chest. She cared for him and his wife. They took care of her and Charles for decades. Could she really have left them and moved to France with Devereux? She was still angry at herself for even considering it.

Devereux. The best lover I ever had. Or was he? After all, she was seventy-seven years old and had many notches on her bedpost since her first love. She wondered if she was simply getting tired of waking up alone in the mornings at her age and made herself believe the stories she told herself about Devereux. But it didn't matter anymore.

"How could someone play with a person's life like this?" she asked.

John regarded her. She was a cunning, deceitful, and demanding woman—many of the same traits as Devereux. *Often, like attracts like.*

Charles's father had been the complete opposite—a farmer, hard worker, and honest. And Mary had only used him to get the child and estate that she wanted.

"At least it appears to have improved your swing. You've not lost a single game."

"I picture his face on every ball."

They laughed. Her cell rang. She glanced at the screen and rolled her eyes. She picked up the phone and tapped the talk icon.

"Hello, darling."

She listened.

"Oh, Dev. I cannot wait to become your bride. Do hurry." She listened. "Still in Boston." She listened. "Well, I understand. Toodles, my love." She hit the end call icon and looked at the phone with a sour face.

"You're quite sure you want to continue with this charade?" John asked.

"Quite sure," Mary said. "Quite sure."

"And you didn't find a single movie the man's ever made?" Emma asked Merek before she took a drink from a paper coffee cup. She frowned at it. "Who made this crap?"

Joey gave her a dirty look, tapped the pencil eraser on a yellow legal pad full of notes and doodles, and leaned back in his chair. They were in his office at the Clintonville Police Department. "I was out of coffee so I just poured water over the grounds from yesterday."

Merek shook his head, "*Nie*. Not a single movie. Not really. Just summaries on his blog, Facebook page, and other posts and tweets he's made, but not where they have played or when the shows aired on TV. I checked many places, IMDb, movie databases, and made calls. You can be anyone you want on the internet."

"Yeah, you can even be dead," she added.

"His cover for marrying rich women all over the world. Explains his attraction to Mary," Joey said.

"What were these women like when you talked to them?" Emma asked.

"Shocked. The ones in France, Brazil, and a few other countries I can't remember, some could barely speak English. I had to talk to them through an interpreter. Took forever. But they're all flying in for the wedding. Can you believe this?" Joey shook his head.

"When will Mr. Stratton be back?" Merek asked.

"In a few weeks. He'll be back in time for the wedding. He took Maggie to New York, then he's going to West Virginia to see Rhonda and fish for a while."

"With Maggie?" Joey asked.

"Yeah. I think he needed some father four-legged-daughter time with her. Plus we needed some time apart."

Joey chuckled. "He probably needed a rest."

Emma stuck out her tongue. "Like you should talk." She stood in front of a picture on the wall of a younger Joey Reed receiving an award from a senator.

"Fishing sounds good. I may want to go down to his place sometime and fish," Joey said.

"You fish, Mr. Joey?" Merek laughed.

"Hey, what's so funny? I can be an outdoor guy. Come on. I'm not a cop *all* the time."

Merek shook his head and laughed harder. "You are no outdoor man. You are too busy with *your* women."

Joey snickered. "You should talk."

Merek gave him a look. They both knew they dated a few of the same dancers from The Messenger Club and never cared to discuss it—an underlying twinge between them.

Emma stopped pacing, turned to Joey, and snapped her fingers. "Didn't you say that the only office Devereux seemed to have was at the wife's place in England? What was her name? Arlonda? Alinda?"

"Amelia."

"Yeah, Amelia. She said he always kept the door locked. Can you get a search warrant and get in there?"

"Could. Really didn't see a need for it, though."

"It couldn't hurt, could it?"

"International dealings," he stopped, shaking his head. "The chief will never go for it. No time. No more resources."

"When did you start telling him everything you do?" She leaned on the desk toward him. "Hmmm?"

Joey eyed her then glanced at Merek. "I need him to sign off to get the ball rolling again."

"Really?" she said sarcastically, crossing her arms in front of her.

Joey frowned. He shook his head, grinning, picked up the phone receiver, and punched in numbers with the eraser end of the pencil. He held his forehead in his hand. "Hey, Paul, Joey Reed. Yeah, long time. Hey look, I'm wondering if you could do me a favor. You have connections with Scotland Yard, right?"

Emma and Merek gave each other a thumbs up.

Charles meandered through the produce section of Weiland's Market with a shopping basket hanging from his arm. He stopped in front of the fish counter.

"Hi, there. What can I get for you today?" the familiar man said with a smile.

"Good afternoon. It all looks wonderful. I know I wish to prepare fish for dinner, but I need to find the proper recipe." He pulled his phone from his belt clip. "I'll return in a few minutes."

"Sure thing."

Charles walked away thinking about salmon, scallops, tuna, and shrimp as he scrolled through a recipe app.

"Hello, Charles."

He had not heard the voice in months, but it was unmistakable. He looked up.

"Ron, how've you been?"

"Fine. You?"

"I'm fine. Thank you."

They stood regarding each other.

"I was searching for a fish recipe," Charles said, holding up his phone before slipping it back into the clip.

"I'm sure you'll find the perfect one. You're an excellent cook."

"Yes. Thank you." Silence. "So, what brings you here?"

"I enjoy shopping here and hadn't been here in a while. It is a drive for me, but it's the only place that carries my favorite pasta."

"I see."

More silence.

"Good luck on your recipe," Ron said. He walked past Charles, his limp barely noticeable, but it was there. The limp was from a car accident Ron was after leaving Charles's house a year ago. Charles never left his side as he nursed Ron back to health.

Charles watched Ron walk out the door. He thought of running after him but returned to his recipe app on the phone instead.

Charles drove from Weiland's and pulled into a gas station. He got out of his Lexus to insert his credit card into the pump. At the next pump, Ron was replacing the gas hose into the cradle. Charles looked at the ground, put his credit card and wallet away, and walked over to Ron, who was putting the cap on his gas tank.

"Twice in one day," Charles said, smiling.

Ron looked up. "Rains it pours, they say."

Charles lowered his head and ran his fingers through his hair. He sighed and looked up at Ron.

"Look, if you're not busy this evening, I did find the perfect fish recipe and ..." He paused and looked at the ground then back at Ron. "I'd like you to come over for dinner."

Ron looked stunned. "Oh, *really*?"

"Yes."

They stood looking at each other in silence.

"Ron, look, I made a terrible mistake and I've always felt horrible about it and later came to regret it more than you'll ever know. I wanted to explain. I called you, but you wouldn't take my calls or answer my texts or emails."

Ron stepped closer to him.

"Am I supposed to apologize to you for that? You're the most pompous man I've ever met. I can't believe I had such strong feelings for you for so many years."

Charles inhaled sharply and took a step back. "Ron, I—"

"Why should I go to your house for dinner? So you can make everything *smooth* for Charles Wellington? Your confession to free you from your guilt? You're so much like your mother. She's a self-centered woman who has no regard for anyone. The apple *doesn't* fall far from the tree, does it?"

"If it makes you feel any better Simon stood me up that night and I've not heard from him since and it's for the best. I'm sorry, I—"

Ron interrupted. "I don't care to hear it."

"Ron, I'm moving to Switzerland in a few weeks. Please have dinner with me. I don't want us to end like this." He shifted his weight from one foot to the other and glanced away.

Ron got in his car, slammed the door, and squealed out of the gas station.

Merek spoke in Polish into his Samsung. "When did this happen?"

He listened. He shook his head. He walked around the living area in his condo. He stopped and looked down through the glass wall at the river. He ran his hand over his head. "She will be okay, then. That is good. When will she go home?"

He walked in circles. "I will call her in the morning when she is home. Thank you for calling." He hit the icon and ended the call.

He stood staring at the river below. He hit another icon on his phone, and the call went into Emma's voice mail. He didn't leave a message.

He called his other brother in Poland and they talked at length about their mother, who had fallen and broken her arm. After the call ended he went to the refrigerator, opened it, and closed it. His cell rang. He picked it up and frowned. *When it pours, it rains in the storm* Merek thought. He took a deep breath and answered.

"Yes, Mr. Calvin."

"I need those changes to the presentation in ten minutes. Send them to me. I can't find Emma. I suppose she's somewhere with Stratton again?" Calvin blurted.

Merek sighed and rolled his eyes. "I will send the presentation now. I gotta scram." He ended the call and walked into his office, sat at his desk, found the presentation and clicked send. "I should tell you where to go, Mr. Calvin Nelson. I am very weary of you."

"Thank you for getting everyone together, Glen. Ribeye on the grill, one of my favorites. This looks wonderful," Stratton said, cutting into his steak.

"We know that, Grandpa," said Todd, Glen and Clarisse's son. "That's why Mom made them."

"Haley, pass the steak sauce to your grandfather," Clarisse said, addressing Todd's younger sister.

"Thank you, honey," Stratton said.

"You're welcome, Grandpa."

Maggie walked around the table, her tail wagging.

"We're glad you brought Maggie," Clarisse said, patting the dog's head.

"I haven't been spending enough time with her lately, so I decided she needed to come with me. We're going fishing next week at the house, just like we used to," Stratton said.

"Dad, we have something we want to discuss with you," Glen said.

"Oh? And what's that?" Stratton said, smiling up at his two children, their spouses, and his four grandchildren.

The room became suddenly still. Ellen and Clarisse shared a look. They both turned toward Glen.

"Dad, we really want you to stop seeing Emma. She's nothing but trouble," Glen said, setting his silverware on his plate.

"That so?" Stratton cut into his steak.

"Daddy, we care about you. You've been shot and kidnapped. I like Emma, but she does seem to, well, you know. Find trouble," Ellen said, refusing to look at her father.

"Mom, Grandpa can date who he wants," Laura piped up.

"Thank you, sweetie," Stratton said. "I agree. Jason, since this appears to be a family reunion turned intervention, what are your thoughts?"

"Me?" Jason asked surprised, pointing at himself. "I think your kidnapping book will be a bestseller," he said.

"See," Stratton said, pointing at Jason with his fork, "that is the spirit of a true journalist." He gave his grandson a nod and a wink.

Jason beamed.

"Dad, we're not kidding around," Glen said. "We're serious. When you get back home, break it off. I'm sorry. It's how we all feel."

The room went quiet.

Ramesh had cooked an Indian dish, and it was going fast. He scooped more onto his plate and said with his Indian accent, "Mr. Reeves, I understand your admiration for this beautiful woman, but she does appear to be dangerous to be around. Do you not agree?"

"Maybe that's part of the attraction," Clarisse said, rolling her eyes.

"You're not having a mid-life crisis, are you, Daddy?" Ellen asked.

Stratton chewed without looking up from his plate. The room remained silent except for the sounds of people eating. Stratton cut another piece of steak and washed it down with a swig of wine. Everyone continued eating until Stratton clattered his silverware onto his plate and threw his napkin on the table. He stood. All eyes were on him.

"I've heard your side. Now, you will listen to mine." He paused. "I love you all and appreciate your concern. True, I nearly lost my life because I was in the wrong place at the wrong time. Period. But I came up here to enjoy being with all of you, not for *this*."

"But—" Ellen said.

"Hold on, honey. I'm not finished.

"I loved your mother and I miss her every day. She's a piece of me just like she's a piece of you. I never thought I'd get over her death. Until Emma Haines walked into my office. That changed my life. I'm happy again. Don't I have a right to be happy?"

"Dad—"Glen said.

"Don't interrupt, me, Son."

Glen shook his head and lowered it.

"No, I'm not having a mid-life crisis. I'm past that. But who are you to tell me who I can date? Answer that."

"Todd, you and Haley go to your rooms, please. You may leave your plates," Clarisse said to her son.

The children slowly stood and walked toward the hallway. "I've never seen Grandpa mad before," Haley whispered to her brother as they left the table.

"Dad, please sit down."

"I think it's best I leave. This conversation is over and it seems to be the only reason why you wanted me here," Stratton said.

"Dad, sit down," Glen demanded.

Stratton glared at his son before he slowly sat back down.

"We know you care about her, but we're family. You're our father, and you've nearly been killed twice because of her. Three times, when you were helping her chase that Calhoon character," Glen said.

"I've nearly been killed more times than I care to remember before I met Emma. She makes me happy. Surprisingly enough, I like being happy."

"We like it, too," Clarisse said. "We're just concerned."

"Can't she just stop chasing bad guys? I thought she worked as a trainer at an insurance company. She sounds like a cop or something. Someone with lots of enemies," Glen said.

"And you don't think a few people I wrote about wouldn't like to see me in the ground?" Stratton asked.

"I get that. But why take more chances? Can't you find someone a little more, I don't know—" Glen said.

"My own age?"

"That doesn't have anything to do with it," Ellen said. "It's just the danger factor."

Stratton looked at the people staring at him. His heart nearly burst from all the love he felt for them, but he was angry and confused.

"Your old man is in love with a woman the same age as his kids. And I'm not sorry. Life threw me a horrible curveball when your mother died. It later hit the ball out of the park when I met Emma."

Ellen got up from her chair, walked behind Stratton, put her arms around his neck, and kissed him on the cheek. "Just be careful, Daddy. We love you."

Glen got up and left the room.

Chapter 15

"Rhonda, you can let go of me now," Stratton said, laughing, pulling away from his office manager. Maggie milled around their legs, thumping them with her tail before she took off for the kitchen.

"It's just awful what you been through. Just awful. I am so thankful that you are here and that they caught that awful man. What was his name again? Coast-er-mister?" She scrunched her face, her orange lipstick wrinkling and her orange eye shadow creasing. She squeezed Stratton's arm.

"Kotmister. Dayton Kotmister."

"And he was the one that Emma put away for burning down his house and made her quit her job? Well that's just awful. And he come after you for revenge on her. Ain't it terrible what people will do to each other? I tell you, Stratton, I can barely watch the news anymore and, well, you know working for a newspaper, well, that's probably not a good thing and I don't go around telling many people I don't watch the news because I have the paper to consider and I don't want people to think bad about the paper.

"So, well, that brings something else up. Well, yes, I want to talk to you about something. You see, we need to put in a column about good news, you know, maybe recipes and maybe even have kids write a column. You know my grandson, Danny. He's all grown up. You should see him. I'll bet he's grown a foot since the last time you saw him and, well, anyway. It's just awful you couldn't be here for his birthday party in April, but then, well, you being kidnapped and all. Well, anyway, my grandson, he's so tall now, well, he's been writing stories. Did I tell you this? Well, he has. And they are good stories, too, Stratton, and well, I think that—"

Stratton leaned against Rhonda's wooden desk and took her by the elbows. "Rhonda, I would love to discuss this with you, but right now I just want to go into my office, go through the mail and my email, and be alone in there for a while. I just want to catch up and relax in my office."

"Yes, yes. I know. I understand." She nodded, shaking her orange plastic earrings.

He patted the sides of her arms. "Could you please get Maggie some food and water and put the bowls in my office beside her bed?"

She grinned and tilted her head. Stratton feared her skinny body would fall over from the weight of her white beehive hairdo. She crossed her arms in front of her orange polyester pantsuit, her orange plastic bracelets clinking. "Well, of course, I will. Where'd she go? And I'll get you a glass of cold tea, too. This July weather is starting to ruin my hair. Do you know how expensive hair spray is? Well, of course, you don't. I doubt Miss

Emma uses hair spray." She patted her hair. "I just made the tea. Now, I didn't put any sugar in it because I know you yankees don't like sweet tea, but I'll—"

"That sounds wonderful. Please, go find Maggie. That's lovely of you, Rhonda."

She gave him another hug and patted his back so hard he nearly burped.

"I am just so glad to see you. Oh, I prayed for you so hard. We all did. Everyone down at the church and everywhere. And everyone in town. And you just wait until you see all the cards, and I'll print out all the emails I received and everyone was just so—"

"That's nice. We'll talk about all this later. Right now, I'm going into my office."

"All right. That's just fine. Yes, you do that. You need some peace and quiet and I'm sure you're going to find it here and, well, I'm just so glad you're back." She turned and called for the golden retriever. "Maggie. Maggie, girl. Where are you?"

Stratton grinned as he shook his head, smoothed his hair, and opened his office door. He walked in and closed it behind him. He stood and admired his large wooden desk, which matched Rhonda's. He spent months looking for those *perfect* desks. He walked around the office and conference table in front of the fire place, stopping in front of each painting of him fishing along the various rivers and streams in the area, admiring each one. Sadness jabbed him as he thought of Ann.

He sat in his quilted, yellow, leather office chair, placed his hands on his desk, and studied them. They were wrinkled with age spots, and his knuckles looked like they were submerged in water for decades. He refocused on the lines, spots, and crevasses of his hands. He thought of the many items they held and touched over the years and lifted them in front of him.

"What am I doing?" he whispered. "She's too young for me. Just too young. Another time. Another place." He placed them back on his desk and looked up at the painting on the facing wall.

"Oh, Ann. Why did you have to leave me? We were perfect. The same age and everything." He shook his head. There was a soft tap on the door.

"Come in."

"Here's Maggie's food," Rhonda said, placing the bowls on the floor beside the bed in front of the fireplace. Maggie trailed close behind, tail wagging. She dived into her food the second the bowl hit the floor.

"I'll be right back with your tea."

"Thank you, Rhonda."

A few minutes later Rhonda returned and set the glass of tea on a coaster in front of Stratton.

"Something troubling you?" she asked.

"I'm fine. Why do you ask?"

She shrugged and sat down in one of the two quilted red leather chairs in front of his desk. "You just seemed so sad just now. I mean, I know you been through so much. It was just awful. Well, now how is that pretty little Miss Emma?" she asked. Her orange lips parted to show all her white dentures in a large smile.

"She's fine. Just fine."

"Why didn't she come with you?"

"We decided we needed a little time to ourselves."

"What's the matter? You two getting along?"

"Yes. Yes, we're getting along fine."

Rhonda frowned. "You two gonna get hitched soon?"

He looked away.

"Something's wrong. What is it? You can talk to me."

Her face grew serious, and she reached over and patted his right hand. Her orange bracelets clanked against the desk and her orange plastic rings clicked together. "Tell me, what's bothering you?"

He leaned back and rocked in his chair, studying the ceiling. He told her about the family discussion the week before. "I think what they were trying to tell me in a nice way is that I'm too old for her. I've been thinking a great deal about it. I don't want to have her looking after me. She's twenty years younger than me and she shouldn't have to be a caregiver to an old man."

"Why, Stratton Reeves, you stop that talk right this second. You ain't sick, are you?"

"No."

"You love her?"

"Yes."

"And she feels the same way?"

"Yes. I believe she does."

"Well, that's all that matters. Family talk or not. Everybody's got a right to live their own lives. And it ain't got nothing to do with aging. It's got everything to do with replacing their momma. Why, something could happen to anyone at any time. There ain't no guarantees in this world. You just got to find love and hang on to it. Is that what's been bothering you?"

"Emma's not replacing their mother."

Rhonda gave him a long look. "You ain't your children. Happens a lot with widowed folks with kids or divorced people with kids that remarry. It's the spot that's being filled by someone else other than the person that should have been there. It's in their head." She tapped the side of her head with a long orange fingernail.

He eyed her. "Why, Rhonda. Not only are you the best office manager in the world, I didn't realize you were also a psychologist." He smiled.

"Oh, now, Stratton. It don't take a psychologist to see what you need to do. You need to marry that girl, right now. I don't know what you been waiting on. I ain't never seen you so happy since you met Miss Emma. Life is short, you know that. You find love, you gotta grab it before it gets away." Her bracelets clattered when she made a grabbing motion with her hands.

Maggie trotted over to Stratton and laid her head on his leg. He scratched her behind the ear and she closed her eyes. "Perhaps you're right."

"I still can't believe you were kidnapped, Mr. Reeves. I wish Emma would've called me. I would've come up to help," John Lawrence said as he cast his bait into the New River. He had been an officer with the Stonefalls Police Department until he and his new wife moved to Charleston after getting a job on their force.

"I appreciate that. It was quite an experience. I'm writing a book about it. Another reason I came down here, to start on it. What's been going on with you?"

"Lou Ann, my wife, we, she, is going to have a baby." He looked giddy.

"That's wonderful news."

"I gotta tell you, Mr. Reeves, I'm scared to death. I mean—a baby—me? I don't know how to be a father."

Stratton laughed. "You'll be a fine father. You and Lou Ann are good people."

"Thank you, sir. But you know what I mean. A baby. I mean. Wow. You know. A real baby." He shook his head, smiling, reeling in another empty hook.

They fished as Maggie ran over the rocks to the edge of the water, wagging her tail, jumping from rock to rock and barking. "Maggie, you better be herding those fish our way," Stratton yelled.

"She's a real pretty dog. Does she get along with Emma's dog?"

"They're buddies. Millie can stand under Maggie, which she does sometimes." Stratton grinned at the thought.

"What kind of dog is Millie?"

"A basset hound. A real sweetie pie."

"Sounds like you and Emma are settling in nice together. You like living in a city again?"

Stratton thought about it for several moments. "I do. But I miss this. More than I realized." He glanced around. A rapid roared upstream. The mountains stood ahead of them and behind them—majestic and green, they held patches of July sun shining on treetops. He gazed at the blue sky. A cloud floated on a summer breeze. Birds sang and a squirrel hopped in the leaves. Two butterflies made their way in front of them, chasing each other in a crazy dance. "Yes, *much* more than I realized."

"Why don't you bring Miss Emma down here more? Or to live? You sure have a nice house here."

"Thank you, John. And those are good questions I've been mulling over a great deal myself."

They fished. Several chickadees chattered in a tree beside them as if they were arguing.

"The last time I fished here I went up that ramp right into Earl Calhoon holding a gun on Chief Davis," Stratton said, turning and nodding behind him. "Still makes me a little nervous. They've not caught him yet, have they?"

Lawrence didn't answer for a long time. "No. He broke clean, and no one has a single lead. When I went to see my uncle, Bill—Chief Davis—about it, he said Calhoon is a crazy, vengeful man, and you two should be careful. My uncle left town. Moved to Florida."

"That's right. I forgot that Davis is your uncle. Rhonda mentioned that he moved." They fished in silence for some time. "You thought he'd come after Emma and me?"

"Yes, sir. When Rhonda called me about your being kidnapped, I thought it was Calhoon."

"Emma thought that, too, at first."

"And she knew it was that Kotmister character from a picture on her phone? That's something else, Mr. Reeves."

"Yes. Amazing, isn't it?"

"How is Miss Emma? She sure is a looker, if you don't mind me saying so."

Stratton laughed. "I don't mind you saying so at all. You're right. She's a beauty." *A young beauty.*

They stood and fished.

"Have you seen Loretta Caldwell since you been in town?" Lawrence asked.

Stratton shook his head. "Not yet. But I'll likely run into her sooner or later. I'll be eating at Nora's. I'll probably run into her there. Hoping for fish tonight though. Have you gotten any good bites?"

"I got something right now," Lawrence said, pulling up on the rod, reeling it in, letting it out, and reeling it in. After about a minute with Stratton cheering him on, he pulled in a huge bass. "Looks like we've got dinner," Lawrence said as Stratton held the net and the fish flopped into it. Lawrence cut the line.

"We'll fry it back at the house," Stratton said as Maggie sniffed the flopping fish.

"Mighty nice of you inviting me down to fish with you, Mr. Reeves."

"You're more than welcome. Want to call it a day?"

"Sure."

They packed their gear and headed back to Stratton's truck, Maggie following. "So is Miss Emma at the house?"

"No, she's at the condo in Clintonville."

"Oh. She busy or something?" Lawrence asked.

"She had some things to do. She'll be down in a few days."

Emma and Stratton were asleep in his king-size bed. The French doors were open, and the curtains fluttered in the June, morning breeze.

The door to the bedroom burst open, and in trotted Maggie and Millie. Maggie jumped on the bed and Millie whimpered, standing on the floor beside Emma.

Stratton jumped as Maggie dug a space between him and Emma. "Maggie, girl." The dog licked him on the face and he laughed, hugging her.

Emma woke up and ran her hand over Maggie's back. She rolled over and patted Millie on the head. "Hey, pup. I'm sorry you're too short to jump up here."

Millie barked several times. "Whoa, someone wants their walk," Emma said. She threw the covers back, got out of bed, and walked naked to the bathroom. Millie followed and Emma shut the door behind them.

"I know. You have to go walk with them, too. Millie has been a bad influence on you," Stratton said, scratching and petting Maggie. She buried her head under his armpit, lifting his arm with her nose, thumping her tail on the pillow-top mattress.

He playfully scratched the dog's head. "I remember when I used to get *you* out of bed and just let you outside. But when you're around the early-morning-riser basset you sing a different tune, don't you? Glad I don't have to walk you at six in the morning." He scratched the dog behind her ears and chuckled.

Maggie stood and romped in the bed, wanting to play. "Calm down. You already have your coffee or what?" Stratton said as he got out of bed. He pulled on his shorts and robe and went into the kitchen. Maggie jumped off the bed and followed, toenails clicking on the floor, tail wagging.

He put on an apron that Emma had bought him and made the coffee before he pulled milk, eggs, and bacon out of the refrigerator. He took a bag of whole wheat flour from a large canister on the bar and set it on the counter.

Emma walked into the kitchen wearing a pair of L.L. Bean shorts and a faded "Life Is Good" kayak T-shirt. She pulled her hair back into a ponytail and put on her *Stonefalls Post* ball cap. She removed the leashes from the hanger on the wall and clipped them to the dogs' collars. "The girls will be back for breakfast in a bit."

"And the cook will have it ready for you upon your return," Stratton said, holding a spatula in the air.

Emma and the dogs bounced down Stratton's front steps. The morning sun warmed the air. Bees were already busy in the flowers over the terrace. A hummingbird flew in for a drink from the trumpet vines. Emma breathed in the clean mountain morning smells, yawned, and stretched.

The dogs led her down the gravel walk, tails wagging and noses to the ground. They moved past the three-car garage down the long paved drive, which ran through the woods about a half-mile to Sewell Mountain, the main road. It was their morning routine to get the paper.

About a quarter mile down the drive the dogs stopped and peered into the woods. Millie barked and whined, followed by Maggie barking and growling. "Anther big buck, girls?" She laughed. "Come on. I'm hungry." The dogs stood fast, staring and barking into the woods more intensely.

"What is it?"

She peered into the trees, trying to fix on what the dogs were seeing. Finally, she gave up. So did the dogs. Everyone walked down the drive, but Maggie and Millie kept their noses in the air, sniffing. Emma hoped it wasn't a skunk—or a bear.

They kept walking, but Emma had to continually prod them along. "Come on. Come on. Stratton's getting breakfast ready for us."

A branch cracked in the woods. The dogs barked and pulled on the leashes. A man dressed in camo walked fast through the woods away from them.

Her skin prickled. *Why would a man be on Stratton's property at six in the morning?*

"Come on. Let's go. Stratton can get the paper later."

Emma and the dogs bustled through the door of the house. Stratton had his keys in his hand. "Where are you going?" she asked.

"I was coming after you," he said.

"Why?"

"The sheriff's department just called. They spotted a strange truck parked at the bottom of the drive and ran the plates."

"We just saw a man in your woods. He was walking away pretty fast, and I don't think he was a hunter. He wasn't carrying anything."

Stratton held her gaze.

"Oh, come on. It wasn't Calhoon."

"The truck was stolen by a man that could fit his description. We'll eat breakfast and then go back to Clintonville."

"You're obsessed with Calhoon. I don't understand it. And I want to stay here for a few more weeks like we planned." She crossed her arms in front of her chest and pouted.

"So do I, but we're leaving."

"I'm surprised you wanted to come back here so soon. You were just here this last weekend. Maybe we should paddle the Mad again before I leave," Charles said to Emma as he paddled his kayak beside her.

She looked up at the slate bank of Alum Cliff. "I wouldn't want to be anywhere else with anyone else. I think I could paddle this every day." She glanced at him and felt a knot in her throat. She gazed down at the water, watching the bow of her boat cut through the stream. She didn't want to cry again.

"Maybe we should build a cabin along here," Stratton said. On the way back from West Virginia to Clintonville, they argued about selling both their homes and moving someplace else. Stratton was insistent, but Emma said she didn't want to talk about it. He even threw in the thought of moving to Switzerland, near Charles. He pulled out all the stops.

"I can't believe they found *Arlene*," Emma said, patting the side of her kayak.

"I think *Arlene* intends to stick with you. West Virginia and now this," Charles said with a smile.

"She's my partner, that's for sure." She stopped and thought of her friend, Arlene and smiled toward the sky. She turned to Stratton and said, "Too bad they never found yours yet, though."

"That's okay. I wanted a new kayak anyway."

"Is that the Jackson model you were researching?" Charles asked.

"Yes."

"It suits you."

"Why thank you, Charles. I do like the green. I think it highlights my eyes."

They laughed.

"It was nice of Merek to shuttle us. Has he ever gone kayaking with you?" Stratton asked.

Charles and Emma laughed.

"Merek's terrified of water. I'm surprised he takes a shower," Emma said.

"And he gets tattoos so often it wouldn't be wise for him to kayak. New tattoos shouldn't be exposed to river water," Charles added.

"Don't take this the wrong way, but I'm surprised that *you* kayak," Stratton said.

Emma snickered. "It is quite an odd hobby for such a high-snootin'-fahhlootin' man like Charles, isn't it? He didn't catch Mary's golf genes."

Charles glanced at her and then at Stratton. He laughed. "I succumbed to the fever the first time Emma and I paddled Hoover Reservoir. Do you remember that day?"

"I sure do. You were scared out of your little designer shorts. 'Am I going to tip? Am I going to tip?' Whiney baby. You must've said that fifty times before you were gliding along like a swan. You're a natural."

"Look," Stratton said, pointing to the sky. Two great blue herons flapped their wide wings going downstream, yellow toes pointed behind them like ballerinas in flight. One of them let out several squawks. Several chickadees flew past them, and a bullfrog sang a low song in the distance.

Emma watched Charles paddle and nearly two decades of memories rushed over her, making her feel lightheaded. He would be moving to Switzerland in just a few weeks.

Stratton glanced over his right shoulder and yelled, "Let's stop for lunch. I'm starving."

"Of course you are," she said.

Merek drove Stratton's black Silverado pickup through the woods and onto the gravel beach along the creek. They had permission to park there from the landowner. He got out, locked the truck, and hid the key where Stratton had told him to place it. He stood and admired the area. The water gurgled through a fallen tree in the middle of the stream. He liked looking at streams and lakes—from a distance. But the memory of falling into the lake *Nieporent Jezioro* as a boy still haunted him, especially around water.

He and his brothers had been horsing around on his uncle's small boat. He turned to look at the water and was pushed overboard. He never knew which of his two brothers pushed him or if they were both behind it. But he could recall it like yesterday. It was one of his first feelings of being perfectly happy before a life-changing event strikes from nowhere.

His uncle had made them all wear life vests. He couldn't swim. The experience had made him terrified of water ever since. He thought it ironic that he should end up so close to someone with such an opposite feeling about water.

A crooked smile crossed his face at the thought of his brothers. They had all been close before he decided to move to America. A shadow from a cloud passed over him. He looked up and sighed.

He walked to his Harley and put on his helmet and gloves. He started the motorcycle and roared up the gravel drive and onto Route 772 toward Chillicothe and Jerry's Pizza. It was only eleven, but he could eat one of their pies anytime.

He walked in, draped his leather biker jacket over the back of a bar stool, sat down, and ordered an all-meat pizza and a glass of water. He dug his Samsung out of the inside pocket of his jacket and set it on the bar. He scrolled through his emails and news feeds, then shut it off. He watched the TV in the corner.

He wondered who dressed the newscaster and thought of stopping by a thrift store on his way home. As he thought about clothes, his Samsung vibrated. He checked the screen. He scowled and checked it again. His eyes widened. He grabbed the phone and hit the talk icon.

"Czesc."

There was silence on the other end of the call.

"Ludnella?"

"Tak," she answered in barely a whisper.

"What is wrong?" he asked in Polish.

"I…"

"Are you all right?"

"Merek, I left my husband."

"What?" He snapped up straight on the stool.

A long pause. "I miss you, Merek. That is why I left my husband."

Merek peered down through the round window at the airport as the plane banked and circled to land in Denver. When it coasted to a stop and the "Unfasten Seatbelt" sign came on, he was the first person digging in the overhead luggage compartment on the full plane. He took out the small carry-on for the older woman sitting beside him and told her he would carry it off the plane for her. He grabbed his worn army-style backpack and threw it over his shoulder.

"That is so nice of you, young man. I'm so sorry, please tell me your name again?"

"Merek. Merek Polanski."

The old lady patted his arm. "You are such a gentleman, Mr. Polanski. There should be more young men like you in this world. I so enjoyed our chat. It made the flight go by so quickly."

"I liked talking with you, too, ma'am."

"I'm sure your girlfriend will be so happy to see you. What a lucky lady. Ludnella, right?"

"*Tak*. Ludnella." His chest grew warm thinking of holding her again. He couldn't help but wonder if she still had her long white hair and wore the shiny sequined tops he adored. Or had she totally changed for her husband?

It seemed a thousand people were standing in the plane ahead of them. She would be waiting for him at the gate. He thought he might explode if the passengers didn't start to move.

He stared down at Mrs. Crawson's white curls atop her little balding head. He wondered about her age. He figured she had to be in her eighties. Such a nice woman. He thought of his mother.

She looked up at him like a small child and smiled. "There certainly are a lot of people on this plane."

He agreed, growing more anxious. Finally, movement at the beginning of the line. When their turn came to leave, Merek helped Mrs. Crawson stand and make her way down the aisle, carrying their luggage. She said she planned to get a taxi to her house from the airport. For some reason, this bothered him.

They walked down the long ramp to the door. Merek kept staring ahead through the tiny opening while Mrs. Crawson held his arm. Finally, they walked into the airport.

Merek searched the crowd right, left, then in front of him. Again. No Ludnella.

"Thank you, Mr. Polanski. I appreciate your company and carrying my luggage for me. It's on wheels so it shouldn't be a problem for me from here."

He glanced through the crowd again. People buzzed around everywhere and the noise made him want to scream. Instead, he looked down at Mrs. Crawson.

"I will get a cab for you. You sit with me. We will wait for Ludnella, then we will get a cab and ride together."

"Oh, that's so thoughtful, but it's not necessary. I'm used to traveling alone since Marvin passed away. If I didn't, I would never see my family."

"No. You come sit. We will wait, and then we will get a cab together."

"Well, I suppose. But only if you let me buy you a snack and something to drink. I'm thirsty. Would you get me a Coke, please?"

Merek led her to two chairs in front of the gate desk and sat her down. "You watch the luggage. I will go get snacks. Look for Ludnella. She is tall, thin, and has long blonde hair to her waist. Lots of earrings and tattoos, like me. Very beautiful. Motion for her and tell her to come wait."

"All right. I'll look for her."

Merek glanced around as he made his way to a food counter. The long line wasn't helping his short patience. *Where is she?*

He bought a Coke, two bottles of water, and two hot pretzels. It took forever for the cashier to ring him through.

He walked back over to Mrs. Crawson and sat down beside her. Merek handed her the pretzel and Coke. She nibbled the pretzel and sipped her drink.

"You should drink water," he said.

She chuckled. "You are like a mother hen, Mr. Polanski."

As he scanned the crowd, he unscrewed the other water bottle and handed it to her, taking her Coke and sitting it on the floor. She took a sip of the water. When Merek wasn't looking, she picked up the Coke.

Nearly an hour passed before Merek put his cell in his biker jacket for the last time and said, "I will go get the cab and take you home."

Mrs. Crawson patted his arm. "No, you will not. You need to stay here and wait on Ludnella. She probably just got caught in traffic."

He shook his head. "She does not answer my calls. She can talk on the phone and drive or pull over. She is not coming."

"She will be here, Mr. Polanski. She will." Her blue eyes sparked like she knew something that he didn't. He sat back in the chair, arms crossed over his chest, frowning.

"She is right, Merek. I am here," came Ludnella's voice from behind them.

He jumped from his chair and turned around. She looked exactly the same in a red sparkling top. She climbed on the chair in front of her, stood on her knees, leaned over, and she and Merek hugged and kissed a long, deep kiss.

"You are here," he whispered in Polish, rubbing his lips across hers and holding her.

"*Tak*," she replied, leaning her forehead against his. "I caught in traffic and phone battery dead. I was afraid you leave."

Mrs. Crawson looked up at Merek, smiling and nodding.

"Oh, excuse me. Ludnella, this is Mrs. Crawson. I met her on the plane."

Mrs. Crawson turned around in her chair. "Pleased to meet you, Ludnella. He certainly was right about you being beautiful." She beamed at them.

Ludnella climbed out of the chair and walked around to stand in front of them, taking Merek's hand.

"You are kind, Mrs. Crawson. Thank you."

Mrs. Crawson stood. "You two have a lot of catching up to do and I need to get home. I have a cat to feed who will be very unhappy if I miss his dinner. I told the neighbors I would be home to feed him. It was so nice meeting you, Mr. Polanski. Ludnella."

Mrs. Crawson started to walk away. "No! We will take you home." He looked at Ludnella questioningly.

"I take taxi," she said, shrugging. "I do not have car."

Merek laughed. "We will all take a taxi and go to an early dinner. On me!" He pulled Ludnella along by the hand and put his arm through Mrs. Crawson's. They walked down the hall together. "This is a wonderful day with the beautiful woman I know and the beautiful woman I just met. We will celebrate."

Chapter 16

MEREK AND LUDNELLA sat in her tiny apartment on the only thing to sit on besides the blow-up mattress—two boxes she hadn't unpacked. He stood, holding his lower back and stretching. "We will not stay here anymore. This place is not good. We will go to a hotel," he said in Polish.

She looked at him like a sad puppy.

"I will take care of you now."

She dropped her head in her hands and began to cry.

"What is wrong, sweetheart? I am here."

"I am so confused."

"About?"

"About what to do. Alex will find me. He will not give divorce, Merek. I do not know what to do."

"Don't get a divorce. You come home with me. I do not care about this mistake marriage. It does not matter to me. You can get a divorce later."

"But it matters to me. I cannot be married to him."

"It does not matter. We will be fine." He stood and rubbed her shoulders. "Let's go eat. We will feel better."

She sniffled and nodded. *"Tak."*

Merek went into the bathroom and shut the door behind him. She stood, gazing out the cracked, dirty windows in the only apartment she could afford. She glanced down as another cockroach scuttled across the floor. She shuddered and cried.

Merek came out of the bathroom and shrugged into his Harley T-shirt. "Where is a good place for breakfast? I am starving." He wore a huge smile.

She shrugged. "I do not know. I only here for a week. I eat cereal."

He frowned and pulled her to him. "You will not have to eat cereal again. I will find us a wonderful place to eat. Then we will go home to Ohio." He kissed her. She pushed him away.

"I am not sure."

"What do you mean?"

She burst into tears again. "Merek, I was not honest with you on phone. But I had to see you."

He held her by the elbows and gazed at her. "What is it?"

She cried harder. "I am to have baby."

He turned and walked away. He stood with his back to her for several moments before he faced her. "Does he know?"

She shook her head and bit her lip. Tears slid through her day-old mascara and thick makeup, streaking her pink face.

Merek paced, rubbing his head. "Why did you not tell me?"

"Because I afraid you would not come."

He glared at her. "We will go eat."

She wiped her face as he led her through the doorway.

On their way down the hall, a hulk of a man walked toward them. He wore a faded T-shirt, dirty jeans, and biker boots. Merek was reminded of a huge bouncer he tangled with when he arrived in America. Ludnella stopped and sucked in air. "Alex."

"What do you think you're doing? Who is *this*?" He studied Merek with a sneer on his face, spreading his feet shoulder width and balling his fists.

Merek pushed Ludnella behind him. "I am Merek Polanski."

"That's my wife, Mr. Polanski. My property. You get away from her right now."

"Alex, how did you find me?"

"You can't do nothing I don't know about."

"I cannot live with you. I am in love with Merek," Ludnella said, peeking around Merek.

Alex's eyes grew wide. "So this is the man from Ohio. The Polish one you met at the dry cleaner. Well, well. She told me all about you when I met her. Crying in her beer that you left her for your boss. But here you are."

Merek stood fast in front of Ludnella. "Let's go inside the apartment and talk this through like adults."

"There's nothing to talk about. We're married. She's my property. You need to leave, right now. Go back to Ohio to, what was her name, Emmie?"

Ludnella squeezed Merek's arm and walked in front of him. "I am not your property," she screamed. "I am a person."

Alex slapped her across the face. Merek jumped on him. The noise in the small hallway sounded like elephants dancing as the men rolled, punched, grunted, kicked, and yelled.

A doorway opened down the hall and slammed shut. A dog yelped. A baby on the floor above them wailed. Ludnella screamed at them to stop fighting.

Alex's lips curled over his teeth as he bent and reached for his left ankle. He straightened. A knife glinted in the light of the bare bulb hanging from its frayed wire overhead.

"No, Alex. No!" Ludnella cried as the men eyed each other like wild beasts. Alex lunged and Merek dodged the blade. He lunged again. The blade sliced Merek's arm and blood splattered the wall.

Ludnella shrieked and ran toward Alex. He pushed her back, and she slammed against the wall and fell. "Stay out of the way, bitch!"

With Alex's attention distracted, Merek side kicked the knife out of his hand. A few punches and Alex lay on the floor, out cold.

Ludnella ran to Alex and put his head in her lap and rocked him. Merek stood panting and bleeding, wiping blood and sweat from his face with the back of his hand before clamping down on the cut in his upper arm.

"Ludnella, come now, let's go."

Tears and mascara streamed down her face and she shook her head. "I cannot leave him. He is the father of my child."

"But you called me to come for you. Let us go, now. Before he wakes up. You are just confused. We can raise the baby."

She sat, shaking her head and crying. "You go back to Ohio. I must stay. I have no choice."

"You have a choice. Come with me. Now. I am leaving, Ludnella. Are you coming?"

She bawled harder and shook her head. Merek turned and walked down the hallway, slamming the door to the apartment building behind him. He took off his T-shirt and wrapped it around the bleeding cut on his arm as he stomped down the crumbling sidewalk. He walked for nearly an hour until he saw a cab and flagged it down. He got in, handed the driver a hundred dollar bill, and told him there was more. He instructed the driver to call the police and send them to Ludnella's address, take him to the nearest grocery store that had a clinic, and wait. He needed a ride to the airport.

"I wish we could've stayed in West Virginia until my birthday, anyway. Millie was getting used to being a mountain basset hound," Emma said, paddling slowly beside Stratton, glancing at the hillside to her left. It was a clear Monday afternoon. An osprey swooped in front of them on Alum Creek Reservoir. "You can't protect me from Calhoon forever. He's probably not even looking for me."

"There's no need to invite trouble," Stratton replied.

"You, of all people, should be used to inviting trouble. You've written some pretty heavy articles about international criminals."

"And as far as I know, they're all still in jail or dead," Stratton said. A fish jumped in front of them, and he wished he had his pole.

A green heron glided through the air, its yellow legs trailing behind its body.

They paddled down Alum Creek into the larger section of the lake, passing turtles lounging in the sun on a dead tree.

They plopped off the log, their heads popping up as Stratton and Emma passed. A red-headed woodpecker pounded away on a tree along the bank. A hawk circled overhead, looking for its next meal.

Stratton paddled next to Emma, reached out and held onto the side of her kayak. "I love you, Emma. You know that."

"It's crossed my mind." She smiled.

"And?"

"You know, since you got back from New York last month you've told me you loved me about fifty times. What's wrong?"

He shook his head.

"I think something's bothering you. Anything happen in New York you forgot to mention?"

Stratton lowered his head. "No."

She examined his hand holding her boat. He was her ageless warrior. Nothing could defeat him. He was her strong soldier, her pillar, teacher, guide, and lover. He brought her comfort, protection, and support. *And I could lose it all in a second.* She flushed as a jolt of fear ran through her like an electric shock. *So much responsibility to put on another for my happiness.* She brushed his cheek with her hand. "Let's go pick up the dogs at Charles's and get over to Merek's."

"She called you and she didn't tell you she was pregnant until you got there? And her husband did that to you?" Emma said, gesturing to Merek's swollen eye and arm with twenty stitches under the bandage. "And I thought you were having a nice vacation in Colorado. You didn't mention you were going to see her, but it's none of my business. She's a real piece of work. That was obvious when she came by the office last year."

Merek set another plate of potato and cheese pierogis and a platter of kielbasa beside the baking dish of kapusta on the table in front of Stratton, Emma, Charles, and Joey. Millie, Maggie, and the boys wandered in, their noses high in the air, wagging their tails as they walked around the glass dining table. After a few rounds, Cleo and Maggie walked over to the glass wall facing the Olentangy River and flopped down on the floor. The sky beyond Merek's balcony was turning pink and blue.

Sam chased Cecil down the hallway, barking. Millie sat on the floor watching Cleo and Maggie until she rolled onto her side and closed her eyes.

"Thank you, Merek. This is all so delicious," Stratton said, spearing more food and placing it onto his plate. Charles and Joey agreed. Emma watched Stratton eat.

"You are all welcome. I am glad everyone could come tonight. You are my friends. I did not want to be alone. I cook food like my mother." He grinned.

Emma reached over and wrapped a hand around his wrist. "This dinner was very nice of you. And I understand. You really had strong feelings for her. I know. But the woman's a nut."

"I saw a new side of her there. Not good. She needs to deal with her problems. Not me. She has called me ten times since I got home. She cries and says she is sorry. I feel bad, but I cannot help her. She is staying with Alex. I am troubled."

"Were you going to bring her back here?" Joey asked between bites.

"I was going to bring her here to live with me."

"And raise her child?" Charles asked.

Merek shrugged. "What else was there to do?"

The room fell silent except for sounds of the dogs playing and friends enjoying a good meal.

"I have to agree with Emma on this one. She sounds like a load, man," Joey finally said.

"She left you, remember?" Emma said.

"Yes." There was a long pause. "Because she was jealous," Merek replied.

"You do have quite a few women hanging around all the time. I mean, I sort of see her point," Emma said.

"What happened to Fantasy?" Joey asked without looking up from his plate. Merek ignored him. He knew Joey liked to watch Fantasy pole dance at the club and they went out a few times. He turned back to Emma.

"Her problem was not the other women, Miss H. It was you."

Emma laughed. "Me?"

He shrugged and cut into his food. "She does not like how I work for you."

"What do you mean?"

"She says you tell me to jump and I jump."

Joey, Charles, and Stratton exchanged glances. Charles coughed into his napkin. Emma shot him a frigid look before turning back to Merek.

"When she wanted you to go with her, you stayed here. You could've gone. You even thanked me for making you a partner in the company and you said she was trouble. You can't blame me."

Merek shrugged and looked at her.

"Is that how you really feel, Merek—that I tell you to jump?"

Merek chewed, not looking up from his food.

"Well, is it?"

"No, Miss H. I like working with you. We are a team."

"You're not just saying that?"

He shook his head. "*Nie*. We train people to crack cases. We find bad guys. We saved Mr. Stratton. All of us. We save lives. It is important work."

Stratton cleared his throat. "And thank all of you, again, by the way," he said between bites. Maggie stood at the table and barked toward Merek as he cut his kielbasa.

"No, Maggie. You know better," Stratton said.

"Merek, are you in love with Ludnella?" Charles asked.

Merek set his knife and fork gently on his plate, finished chewing, and propped his chin on his hand. "*Tak*."

"Then maybe you should grab on and hold on to her, no matter what," Stratton said.

"Whoa, Dr. Phil. What brought that on?" Emma asked, laughing.

He chewed and swallowed. "Sometimes love isn't wrapped up in a pretty package with a bow. It has challenges. That's all I'm saying, dear."

"Don't I know it. All relationships have challenges," Joey said, shaking his head.

"They most certainly do," Charles agreed.

Joey pointed his fork at Emma and Stratton. "I mean, okay, look at your age difference, for example. I mean, it's cool, you know that, and you seem to get along great and all, but ... Never mind."

Emma turned to Stratton. "Is our age difference a problem for you?"

Stratton scooped up more kapusta.

"Well?" she asked again.

He chewed, lifted his eyebrows, and gave her a wide-eyed look.

Merek raised his wine glass. "Tonight, we celebrate friendship."

Emma sat on her couch with her iPad propped on her knees, flipping through her kayak trip picture albums at two in the morning. She couldn't sleep.

She watched Millie snoring in her bed beside the gas fireplace, her paws occasionally twitching. Emma wondered what she was dreaming. She felt the love for the basset swell in her chest.

She glanced past Millie to the fireplace. This past winter, she loved cuddling with Stratton, Millie, and Maggie in front of it, where unlit candles now stood behind the screen. Several evenings she and Stratton would have hors d'oeuvres of wine and cheese before they went into the kitchen and cooked dinner together. A few times they delayed dinner, their kissing leading to lovemaking.

The air conditioner hummed, taking out the July heat and humidity, keeping her condo comfortable. She glanced at the bookcases in the dining room near the window seat. They were full of her favorite books, knickknacks, rocks from rivers, and several pictures in unique frames she collected over the years. As much as she loved Stratton's house overlooking a stream and the mountains in West Virginia, this was home—her comfy Clintonville condo.

She purchased it herself soon after she was hired at Matrix Insurance. Mr. Matrix had introduced her to his Realtor, and it only took a few minutes to walk through the empty condo and fall in love with it.

After she started H.I.T., she discovered the perfect office in a quaint brick building, an easy walk from her front door.

She thought about her life. She was content and happy for the past twenty-four years, working in claims and then training insurance fraud investigators at Matrix, making Merek a full partner of H.I.T. and kayaking around the country. Then she and Charles had run into Earl Calhoon on the New River a year ago, and over the course of that event, she met Stratton. She glanced up as his snores seeped through the ceiling.

He was talking more and more about them selling their homes, building one together or moving someplace else. He avoided the word marriage.

She flipped through the picture albums, sipping a glass of Côtes du Rhône. She lifted her glass and examined the wine, remembering Charles leaning over the table to pour her first taste of it into her glass at The Worthington Inn.

"You simply must try this wine, Emma. Tom recommended it to us the last time we were here and it is divine. You'll enjoy it."

Simon had agreed. She took a sip and had been drinking it ever since. The three of them had toasted, celebrating Simon's birthday.

She swirled the liquid and took another sip. She lowered the glass and gazed into it again.

She pictured Charles paddling toward her as he blasted through the first rapid on the New River, his gleaming smile under his salt and pepper mustache tinged with drops of water. He wore his sparkle blue helmet, which matched his blue paddle and boat. She thought of the many river trips they paddled together all over the country. And now he was moving—leaving her.

So many things have changed.

Maggie walked into the room and laid her head in Emma's lap. Millie looked up from her bed, yawned, stood, shook, stretched while wagging her tail, and joined them.

Emma put her iPad on the end table and sat on the floor against the couch. The dogs lay on either side of her. Millie rolled onto her back, begging for a belly rub. Emma scratched Millie's tummy and Maggie's head and chest.

"You girls should be glad you're not human. You don't have to go to work. You don't have to deal with relationships. You don't have to deal with snoring, even though, Millie, you give Stratton a run for his money."

Millie thumped her tail on the floor, looking at her stoically, then pointed her nose toward the ceiling. Emma laughed.

"Yeah, well … You don't have to have your heart broken when your best friend decides to move across the globe. But you'll probably miss the boys, I guess."

The dogs climbed into her lap and licked her face.

It was a breezy, August Saturday morning and the weather couldn't have been kinder. The flowers seemed to sway in a dance as the smell of a gentle summer day floated in the air. Emma and Stratton sat holding hands in the fourth row of dozens of white folding chairs in Mary's yard, most already full.

Emma's brunette hair was swooped in an up-do held by a spray of flowers. She wore a white shift dress and matching jacket. Her white stilettos were a bit difficult to navigate in on the carpeted lawn, but she did fine, hanging onto Stratton's strong arm.

Stratton wore a light gray pinstripe suit and a starched pink shirt with a matching pink kerchief peeking out of the front jacket pocket. His diamond tie clip that Glen and Ellen gave him during his last visit, flashed in the sun as he turned to take in the scene.

Charles wore a white linen Armani suit, a yellow silk shirt, and purple tie. He walked past them, his iPhone to his ear, and went into the house.

Merek sported a white leather jacket, white linen shirt and pants, and a pair of bright blue leather loafers, no socks. He sat on the other side of the aisle from Emma and Stratton, flipping through emails and Facebook on his phone, while keeping a designer-sunglass-covered eye on the gazebo in front of him.

"This should be something else," Emma whispered to Stratton as people found their seats.

He squeezed her hand.

"You know, I'm glad you're such a tough old bird. I needed a date for this wedding. I can't believe it's finally happening."

"Joey has so much dirt on ole Dev, it'll bury him deep. We'll see how this goes. I think he'll run," Stratton said.

"Maybe. Joey told Merek and Charles to be ready for anything. I just hope he's not packing."

"We all do. But Mary and Joey believe he doesn't suspect a thing. Let's hope they're right."

Women wore fancy sundresses and bonnets. Men wore lightweight suits. Several actors, celebrities, performers, and professional golfers slipped in as their security lined up along the back of the crowd trying, but failing, to be inconspicuous.

"Oh, my. I had no idea she'd be here. I just saw her on Broadway while I was in New York. Her performance was splendid. And, is that …? Why, it *is*!" Stratton said. "I had no idea Mary knew so many famous people."

"Yeah. Charles has told me about it for years," she said. "Mary runs in many circles."

A canopy of flowers covered a long trellis above the white carpet leading to the gazebo, where a string quartet played soft music. When the band began playing the wedding march, everyone stood.

Women dressed in knee-length navy designer strapless dresses walked down the carpeted aisle, throwing blossoms and smiling. They lined up along the front left side of the gazebo, followed by Devereux and, finally, Mary. Her toned and tanned body glowed around a white strapless dress trimmed in blue satin. Sitting on her head, a small blue hat tilted to the left. A blue veil covered her face above a diamond necklace and matching drop earrings. She was stunning as she strode down the carpet through the crowd.

News reporters and paparazzi cameras clicked and whirred as Mary stopped and posed several times, basking in every moment.

Devereux smiled at his bride while Charles gave her hand to him and they turned to face the guests. The minister stood to their side on the step below them and motioned for everyone to be seated. The music stopped and the minister spoke, stopped, and nodded toward Devereux.

Devereux took Mary's hands and gazed into her eyes. "In you, my lovely Mary, I have never met such a free-spirited and beautiful woman. I love you with all my heart," he said, his French accent, deep and romantic.

Emma squeezed Stratton's arm as Charles gave them a wide-eyed look as he stood beside Mary. Merek sat at attention.

The minister looked at Mary.

She lifted her veil and took both his hands. "And you, Devereux, were the love of my life until I found out about your other wives, your lies and deceit, and your Ponzi scheme. I vow to stop you today from hurting any more innocent people." Mary clamped hard onto his hands then pushed him away. The cameras went wild.

The audience fell silent. Several people gasped. A woman asked, "What did she say?" Whispers floated through the crowd.

Joey came from around the side of the gazebo as the minister stepped away. Joey took Mary's place, cuffing Devereux. "You are under arrest for bigamy and grand theft. You have the right to remain silent. Anything you say can and will be used against you in a court of law …"

Devereux stood speechless, as Amelia and his wives from around the world stood. They pulled back the veils from their hats and glared at him.

People watched with gaping mouths as Mary walked past them, head held high, and stopped on the white carpet. She turned in a circle to the audience and yelled, "Love wild, and strong, and cautious, while always protecting your heart and yourself." She turned and took one last look at Devereux and yelled, "Let the party begin!"

She walked to Emma and Stratton and handed her the bouquet of flowers. "Put these in water, will you, please, dear?" She kissed Emma on the cheek and took Charles's arm as he came up beside her.

As the police loaded Devereux into a cruiser, more band members took the stage with electric guitars, drums, keyboards, and singers. Chords blasted from the amplifiers.

Mary whooped, kicked off her white heels, turned to Charles, and they began to dance.

Stratton, Emma, Charles, Merek, and Joey sat at table in Dante's Pizza on Indianola Avenue in Clintonville. Stratton picked up another piece of pizza and took a bite.

"I still can't believe you busted the biggest Ponzi scheme ever. I'm so proud of you. Who would've known that he was doing that, *too*?" Emma said to Joey as she reached over the table and patted his arm.

Joey raised his beer for a toast. They all raised their glasses. "Who indeed? But if you and Merek hadn't pushed me to make that call, I doubt I'd ever gone after him other than on the bigamy charges. To you guys."

"No, you would've," she said. "To Detective Joey Reed."

Glasses and bottles clinked, and the waitress came to the table to see if anyone needed anything. They said they needed another round of drinks and pizza as Stratton picked up the last piece from the pan in front of them, before the waitress carried it away.

"How do you do it?" Emma asked him.

"What?"

Merek burst into laughter. "You eat like a big horse."

"Do I? Me?" he said between bites.

Everyone laughed.

"But you still look like a handsome model," Emma said, wrapping her arm around his shoulders and pulling him close to give him a kiss on the cheek. He smiled and chewed.

"So what exactly did they find in Devereux's office in London?" Charles asked.

"A ton of phony statements he typed on his computer to some of the biggest businesspeople, celebrities, rock stars—you name it. I can't talk about the details until the trial's over, but it's a mess. It'll take years to straighten out. That Devereux is one slimy dude."

"He's very charismatic. They're the worst kind," Stratton said, licking his fingers.

"Look who's talking," Emma said, picking up a napkin and wiping red sauce off his chin.

"What is this? Pick on Stratton Reeves night?"

"Shhhh ... Are you going to tell them your big news?" she asked him.

"My news? Ah, yes. I received the signed contract back, so, yes, I can share."

"Listen to this, guys." She turned back to Stratton. "Sorry, go ahead, tell them."

"Are you sure, dear? Or would you like to tell them?"

"I'm sorry. Go ahead," she said.

"All right. I've received an ample advance to write a book about my kidnapping and the Kotmister family. I can't wait to give Dayton the first signed copy."

"So your little scheme to save your skin while you were being held hostage turned out to be a reality." Joey said. "That was pretty smart on your part. Did you really think Kotmister would fall for it?"

Stratton leaned back in his seat. "One thing I've learned over the years as a journalist is that many egotistical and disturbed people would love to see their life story in a book. They want to tell their side, show people their reasons, how smart they are, win people over. To be accepted, like anyone, I suppose. I really had nothing else to offer him except that. I bet on his ego and, thankfully, I won. Here I am."

"That is cool, Mr. Stratton," Merek said. "Are we in the book, too?" He sat forward, pointing at himself, his piercings in his ears, nose, eyebrows, and the tiny silver ring in his lower lip catching the light.

"Of course. I mean you helped spring me, right?" Stratton chuckled.

"We did spring you," Emma said. "With a little help, I guess."

"Not to change the subject, but does Devereux have a last name?" Charles asked.

"He has plenty of names. He and his friends, Regal and Leslie, seem to have quite the track record. International crimes. And he had just gotten engaged to a rich widow in Boston the week before his wedding here. She was full of cash and lonely."

Emma watched Charles pick up his wine glass and took another sip with his familiar grace and ease. *How will I live without him in my life?* She took a drink from her wine glass. She wasn't about to ruin the jovial mood of the evening with tears.

"I have good news, too," Merek jumped in.

"Do share," Stratton said.

"The New York woman at the gas station in Kentucky called. The singing woman. Natalie. Very beautiful. So beautiful."

"Oh, yeah. I remember you told me about Natalie. But you left out the beautiful part," Emma said.

Merek smiled and continued. "She called to thank me. She said she is going back to college and majoring in music and voice."

"Beautiful singing woman? College?" Joey asked with a confused look on his face.

"When I helped look for Mr. Stratton in Kentucky I stopped at an old gas station in the mountains. The woman there, Natalie, sang so beautifully with the radio. And she said she wished she would've finished college. I told her she should. She lives in Manhattan. She was there to help her brother with the old family store. Many lining silver to the clouds."

"Oh. Okay. Got it. I think. I've got some lining silver news myself. I didn't get saved from a kidnapper, live through being run over by a truck, receive an ample book advance, or send anyone to college, but I did get a promotion," Joey said.

Everyone cheered.

Chapter 17

A JET SLICED through the sky outside the window behind Emma and Charles at Port Columbus International Airport.

"I'm sorry about Simon," Emma said.

"Yes. But now I know. I have closure."

"He loved you, Charles. You gave him a beautiful service. I've never seen so many people."

Charles took a deep breath. "Yes. I believe he would've been pleased."

"And they confessed. Murder, kidnapping, money laundering. Stratton got Dayton's confession on that recorder. And they found all those notebooks in José's house in Spain, too. Written confessions about everything for the past five years. Right there. They'll never get out of prison."

In 2009, Dayton Kotmister told Simon Johnson that if he didn't move to Spain and never contact Charles again, he would kill Charles. Simon went to Spain, but escaped three years later back to Clintonville, planning to explain everything to Charles. But he never got the chance.

José confessed that he shot him on Dayton's orders and buried the body outside of town. Every step taken was in one of José's notebooks, in a letter to his mother, begging forgiveness while explaining the necessity of it. Everything had checked out.

"So Mary is in Australia on a golf tour?"

"Yes, and it was perfect timing. We said our goodbyes last week. She still doesn't know I've been seeing Father."

"We'll be there for Christmas just like we planned. Okay?" Emma said, sniffling and brushing tears from her cheeks.

"Yes, absolutely. I'm expecting you. It's only four months. It'll take you at least that long to pack. Bring Millie and Maggie, too."

They grabbed each other and held on.

"Emma, I've got to go. My plane is boarding," he whispered in her ear.

"I know." They pulled away and held hands. Emma could feel his left pinkie twitching.

"I love you," he said.

"I love you, too."

They hugged. Without making eye contact they turned from each other and walked opposite directions. Neither of them looked back.

Charles met his father at the boarding gate and they walked onto the plane as Emma walked down the hallway with Stratton and Merek.

"Miss H., Mr. Stratton, I would like a hot pretzel. You want one?" Merek asked.

"No, thanks," she said, shaking her head.

"That sounds wonderful. I'll take one. With mustard, please," Stratton said.

Merek headed for the pretzel stand, his head down, hands shoved in his leather pants pockets.

Stratton put his arm around Emma's waist and they walked to the window. Charles's plane to Switzerland backed from the terminal, sped down the runway, and disappeared into the summer sky.

Around the corner, Merek walked toward them carrying two hot pretzels and a one-way ticket to Poland.

TO BE CONTINUED

About the Author

Trudy Brandenburg is an avid kayaker and writer. Over the past fourteen years, she has paddled on many rivers and lakes, the North Atlantic and North Pacific oceans, and the Gulf of Mexico. She is a member of the Southern Ohio Floaters Association (SOFA) paddling club, based in her hometown of Chillicothe, Ohio.

Her writing has appeared in various publications, including *The Columbus Dispatch*, *614 Magazine*, and an essay in the *Chillicothe Gazette 2014 My Scioto Valley Magazine*, which received an honorable mention. She's been a researcher and writer at an insurance company for the past twenty-three years.

This is her third novel in "The Emma Haines Kayak Mystery Series." The other two are *Nighthawks on the New River* and *Peacocks on Paint Creek*. She is currently working on the fourth book in the series.

When she's not kayaking or writing or reading or playing her piano or creating her designer greeting cards, she's strolling through Clintonville, Ohio, where she's lived for nearly thirty years.

Trudy may be contacted for speaking engagements, writing class instruction, and book signings at the "Contact" tab at the link below.

http://trudybrandenburg.wixsite.com/trudybrandenburg

Made in the USA
Monee, IL
14 July 2023

38697959R00146